D0115161

About Time

Time

Time

Twelve Stories by

Jack Finney

A Fireside Book
Published by Simon & Schuster, Inc.
New York

First Fireside Edition, 1986
Published by Simon & Schuster, Inc.
Simon & Schuster Building
Rockefeller Center
1230 Avenue of the Americas
New York, New York 10020
FIRESIDE and colophon are registered trademarks
of Simon & Schuster, Inc.
Designed by Karolina Harris
Manufactured in the United States of America
Pbk. 1 2 3 4 5 6 7 8 9 10
Library of Congress Cataloging in Publication Data
Finney, Jack.
About time.
"Fireside book."
Stories originally published in his The Third level
and I love Galesburg in the springtime.
Contents: The third level—I love Galesburg in
the springtime—Such interesting neighbors—[etc.]
1. Fantastic fiction, American. I. Title.
PS3556.I52A6 1986 813'.54 86-10077
ISBN: 0-671-62887-9 Pbk.

Acknowledgments

The stories in this book have been previously published as follows:

"The Third Level," "Such Interesting Neighbors," "Of Missing Persons," "I'm Scared" and "Second Chance" were originally published in *The Third Level,* Copyright 1957 by Jack Finney, copyright renewed 1976 by Jack Finney. Originally published by Rhinehart & Company, Inc.

"I Love Galesburg in the Springtime," "The Coin Collector," "Lunch-Hour Magic" (original title, "Love, Your Magic Spell is Everywhere"), "Where the Cluetts Are," "The Face in the Photo," "Home Alone" (original title, "The Intrepid Aeronaut"), and "Hey, Look at Me!" were originally published in *I Love Galesburg in the Springtime,* Copyright © 1962 by Jack Finney. Originally published by Simon & Schuster, Inc.

Contents

The Third Level

The presidents of the New York Central and the New York, New Haven and Hartford railroads will swear on a stack of timetables that there are only two. But I say there are three, because I've *been* on the third level at Grand Central Station. Yes, I've taken the obvious step: I talked to a psychiatrist friend of mine, among others. I told him about the third level at Grand Central Station, and he said it was a waking-dream wish fulfillment. He said I was unhappy. That made my wife kind of mad, but he explained that he meant the modern world is full of insecurity, fear, war, worry and all the rest of it, and that I just want to escape. Well, who doesn't? Everybody I know wants to escape, but they don't wander down into any third level at Grand Central Station.

But that's the reason, he said, and my friends all agreed. Everything points to it, they claimed. My stamp collecting, for example; that's a "temporary refuge from reality." Well, maybe, but my grandfather didn't need any refuge from reality; things were pretty nice and peaceful in his day, from all I hear, and he started my collection. It's a nice collection, too, blocks of four of practically every U. S. issue, first-day covers, and so on. President Roosevelt collected stamps, too, you know.

Anyway, here's what happened at Grand Central. One night last summer I worked late at the office. I was in a hurry to get uptown to my apartment so I decided to take the subway from Grand Central because it's faster than the bus.

Now, I don't know why this should have happened to me. I'm just an ordinary guy named Charley, thirty-one years old, and I was wearing a tan gabardine suit and a straw hat with a fancy band; I passed a dozen men who looked just like me. And I wasn't trying to escape from anything; I just wanted to get home to Louisa, my wife.

I turned into Grand Central from Vanderbilt Avenue, and went down the steps to the first level, where you take trains like the Twentieth Century. Then I walked down another flight to the second level, where the suburban trains leave from, ducked into an arched doorway heading for the subway—and got lost. That's easy to do. I've been in and out of Grand Central hundreds of times, but I'm always bumping into new doorways and stairs and corridors. Once I got into a tunnel about a mile long and came out in the lobby of the Roosevelt Hotel. Another time I came up in an office building on Forty-sixth Street, three blocks away.

Sometimes I think Grand Central is growing like a tree, pushing out new corridors and staircases like roots. There's probably a long tunnel that nobody knows about feeling its way under the city right now, on its way to Times Square, and maybe another to Central Park. And maybe—because for so many people through the years Grand Central *has* been an exit, a way of escape—maybe that's how the tunnel I got into . . . But I never told my psychiatrist friend about that idea.

The corridor I was in began angling left and slanting downward and I thought that was wrong, but I kept on walking. All I could hear was the empty sound of my own footsteps and I didn't pass a soul. Then I heard that sort of hollow roar ahead that means open space and people talking. The tunnel turned sharp left; I went down a short flight of stairs and came out on the third level at Grand Central Station. For just a moment I thought I was back on the second level, but I saw the room was smaller, there were fewer ticket windows and train gates, and the information booth in the center was wood and old-looking. And the man in the booth wore a green eyeshade and long black sleeve protectors. The lights were dim and sort of flickering. Then I saw why; they were open-flame gaslights.

There were brass spittoons on the floor, and across the station a glint of light caught my eye; a man was pulling a gold watch from his vest pocket. He snapped open the cover, glanced at his watch, and frowned. He wore a derby hat, a black four-button suit with tiny lapels, and he had a big, black, handle-bar mustache. Then I looked around and saw that everyone in the station was dressed like eighteen-ninety-something; I never saw so many beards, sideburns and fancy mustaches in my life. A woman walked in through the train gate; she wore a dress with leg-of-mutton sleeves and skirts to the top of her high-buttoned shoes. Back of her, out on the tracks, I caught a glimpse of a locomotive, a very small Currier & Ives locomotive with a funnel-shaped stack. And then I knew.

To make sure, I walked over to a newsboy and glanced at the stack of papers at his feet. It was The *World;* and The *World* hasn't been published for years. The lead story said something about President Cleveland. I've found that front page since, in the Public Library files, and it was printed June 11, 1894.

I turned toward the ticket windows knowing that here—on the third level at Grand Central—I could buy tickets that would take Louisa and me anywhere in the United States we wanted to go. In the year 1894. And I wanted two tickets to Galesburg, Illinois.

Have you ever been there? It's a wonderful town still, with big old frame houses, huge lawns and tremendous trees whose branches meet overhead and roof the streets. And in 1894, summer evenings were twice as long, and people sat out on their lawns, the men smoking cigars and talking quietly, the women waving palm-leaf fans, with the fireflies all around, in a peaceful world. To be back there with the First World War still twenty years off, and World War II, over forty years in the future . . . I wanted two tickets for that.

The clerk figured the fare—he glanced at my fancy hatband, but he figured the fare—and I had enough for two coach tickets, one way. But when I counted out the money and looked up, the clerk was staring at me. He nodded at the bills. "That ain't money, mister," he said, "and if you're trying to skin me you won't get very far," and he glanced at the cash drawer beside him. Of course the money in his drawer was old-style bills, half again as big as the money we use nowadays, and different-looking. I turned away and got out fast. There's nothing nice about jail, even in 1894.

And that was that. I left the same way I came, I suppose. Next day, during lunch hour, I drew three hundred dollars out of the bank, nearly all we had, and bought old-style currency (that *really* worried my psychiatrist friend). You can buy old money at almost any coin dealer's, but you have to pay a premium. My three hundred dollars bought less than two hundred in old-style bills, but I didn't care; eggs were thirteen cents a dozen in 1894.

But I've never again found the corridor that leads to the third level at Grand Central Station, although I've tried often enough.

Louisa was pretty worried when I told her all this, and didn't want me to look for the third level any more, and after a while I stopped; I went back to my stamps. But now we're *both* looking, every week end, because now we have proof that the third level is still there. My friend Sam Weiner disappeared! Nobody knew where, but I sort of suspected because Sam's a city boy, and I used to tell him about Galesburg—I went to school there—and he always said he liked the sound of the place. And that's where he is, all right. In 1894.

Because one night, fussing with my stamp collection, I found—well, do you know what a first-day cover is? When a new stamp is issued, stamp collectors buy some and use them to mail envelopes to themselves on the very first day of sale; and the postmark proves the date. The envelope is called a first-day cover. They're never opened; you just put blank paper in the envelope.

That night, among my oldest first-day covers, I found one that shouldn't have been there. But there it was. It was there because someone had mailed it to my grandfather at his home in Galesburg; that's what the address on the envelope said. And it had been there since July 18, 1894—the postmark showed that—yet I didn't remember it at all. The stamp was a six-cent, dull brown, with a picture of President Garfield. Naturally, when the envelope came to Granddad in the mail, it went right into his collection and stayed there—till I took it out and opened it.

The paper inside wasn't blank. It read:

941 Willard Street
Galesburg, Illinois
July 18, 1894

Charley:

I got to wishing that you were right. Then I got to believing you were right. And, Charley, it's true; I found the third level! I've been here two weeks, and right now, down the street at the Dalys', someone is playing a piano, and they're all out on the front porch singing, "Seeing Nellie Home." And I'm invited over for lemonade. Come on back, Charley and Louisa. Keep looking till you find the third level! It's worth it, believe me!

The note is signed *Sam.*

At the stamp and coin store I go to, I found out that Sam bought eight hundred dollars' worth of old-style currency. That ought to set him up in a nice little hay, feed and grain business; he always said that's what he really wished he could do, and he certainly can't go back to his old business. Not in Galesburg, Illinois, in 1894. His old business? Why, Sam was my psychiatrist.

I Love Galesburg in the Springtime

". . . and in the summer when it sizzles, and in the fall, and in the winter when the snow lies along the black branches of the trees that line its streets."

—Lines tapped out on his typewriter, when he should have been writing up the Soangetaha Country Club dance) by Oscar Mannheim, Galesburg, Illinois, *Register-Mail* reporter.

I didn't make the mistake—he'd have thrown me down the elevator shaft—of trying to see E. V. Marsh in his room at the Custer. I waited in the lobby, watching the coffeeshop, till he'd finished breakfast and was sipping his second cup of coffee before I braced him, walking up to his table smiling my lopsided, ingratiating, Jimmy Stewart smile.

When he learned I was from the paper he tried to fend me off. "I've got nothing for you," he said, shaking his head. He was a heavy man in his fifties, with straight thinning hair. "There's no story. There just won't be any factory of mine in Galesburg, that's all. I'm leaving this town on the first train I can get."

"Well, I'm sorry to hear that," I said untruthfully, and dragged up a chair from an adjacent table. Straddling it, I sat down facing Marsh across the chair back, chin on my folded arms. "But that's not why I'm here," I added softly, and waited. I'm a tall, bone-thin man; my pants legs flop like sails when I walk. I have a bony face, too, more or less permanently tanned, and straight Indian-black hair; and I'm still young, I guess. People generally like me all right.

But Marsh was mad now, his face reddening, his jaw muscles working; he knew what I meant. I glanced quickly around the room; it was still early and there were only a few people here. We were at a corner table looking out on Kellogg Street; no one was near us.

Leaning closer to Marsh's table, my chair legs tilting forward, I said, "I'd rather get the story from you as it really happened than try to piece it together from a lot of half-true rumors floating around town."

He glared. Then he leaned toward me, voice quiet but furious. "I wasn't drunk. I can tell you that!"

"I'm sure you weren't. Tell me about it." And because I'm a reporter, he did.

He sighed a little, going through the motions of reluctance, but actually—and this is usually true—he was glad to talk now that he had to or thought he did. Ilene brought over the coffee I'd ordered when I walked into the room and I picked up my cup and tasted it; the coffee's good at the Custer. Then I dropped my chin to my folded arms, feeling alive and eager, anxious to listen. Because the only reason I was here, the only reason I'm a reporter at all, was simple curiosity. Haven't you ever wished it were somehow possible to cross-examine an absolute stranger about something none of your business but damned interesting all the same? Well, think it over—if you're a reporter, you can. There's no law says it has to be printed.

"I had two drinks before dinner," Marsh said. "We all did. We ate up in my suite—the property owner, a Chamber of Commerce man, an attorney from the city, and a couple of councilmen. If you want a list of their names, ask them for it. After dinner most of us had a brandy. But we sat at the table from seven till ten and whatever drinks I had were spread over a considerable time; I wasn't drunk or even close." Marsh shrugged impatiently. "We worked things out—the price of the factory site, option terms, the probable contractor. Both councilmen and the attorney assured me there'd be no trouble about changing zoning restrictions, if necessary, or running my trucks down Broad Street to the Santa Fe depot. All friendly and pleasant." Marsh took a cigar from the breast pocket of his suit coat and offered it. I shook my head and he began pulling off the cellophane wrapper. "But I like to sleep on a deal of any importance and told them I'd think it over. They left about ten and I took a walk."

Marsh stuck the unlighted cigar in his mouth, bulging one cheek out, and leaned toward me. "I always do that," he said angrily. "I take a walk and go over the facts in my mind; then home to bed, and when I wake up in the morning I usually know what I want to do. So I left the hotel here, walked up Kellogg to Main Street, then over to the Public Square, and when I came to Broad Street I turned up it. Not because the proposed factory site was on Broad; it's way out near the city limits, a dozen blocks or more, and I wasn't planning to walk that. Besides I'd been all over the site that day and I couldn't have seen anything in the dark anyway. But Broad was as good a street as any other to walk along." Marsh brought out matches, prepared to strike one, then sat staring at the tabletop instead. "At that, I walked a lot farther than I meant to. Pleasant street." He struck his match and looked up at me for comment, sucking the flame onto the cigar end.

"It's beautiful," I said, nodding. "All those streets—Broad, Cherry, Prairie, Kellogg, Seminary, and all the others—are beautiful," and I was remembering the day my father, mother, sister, and I got off the train from Chicago at the Q depot. We rode through Galesburg then, in a taxi, to the house my father had bought on Broad Street. The driver took us up Seminary first, from the depot, then along Kellogg, Prairie, and Cherry—a few blocks on each street—before turning onto Broad. I was six and as we rode something in me was responding to the town around us, and I began falling in love with Galesburg even before we reached our house. It happened completely, love at first sight, just north of Main Street when I first saw the thick old trees that line the streets of Galesburg, arching and meeting high overhead as far as I could see. We moved along under those new-leaved trees and the first warm-weather insects were sounding and the street was dappled with shade and sun, the pattern of it stirring as the trees moved in the late spring air. Then I heard our tires humming with a ripply sound that was new to me, and saw that the street was paved with brick. I guess that's not done any more; nowadays, it's concrete or asphalt, never brick.

But a great many Galesburg streets are still brick-paved, and some of the curbing is still quarried stone. And in the grassways beside those brick-paved streets there still remain stone curbside steps for entering or leaving carriages. Near them—not added for quaintness' sake, but remaining from the days when they were put there for use—is an occasional stone or cast-iron hitching post. Back past the grassways and the sidewalks (of brick, too, often), and beyond the deep front lawns, rise the fine old houses. Many are wood, often painted white; some are brick or time-darkened stone; but—there along Cherry, Broad, Prairie, Academy, and the other old streets—they have the half comically ugly, half charming look, made of spaciousness, dignity, foolishness, and conspicuous waste, that belongs to another time.

I mean the curved bay windows with curving window glass; the ridiculous scroll and lathework at the eaves; the rounding, skyrocket-shaped tower rooms with conical roofs; the stained-glass windows (one of them, on Broad Street, I think, an actual pastoral scene); the great, wide front porches; the two stories with an attic above; the tall, lean windows beginning just over the floor. You know what I mean, you've seen them, too, and admired them wryly; the kind old houses of other and better times. Some of them are sagging and debauched, decrepit and in need of paint. Some have been modernized, and there are new houses among them. These aren't museum streets but streets where human beings live. But many of the old houses here in Galesburg stand as always, occasionally the families living in them descendants of the families who built them in the deep peace of the eighties, nineties, the turn of the century, and the early twenties.

"Broad is a nice street, all right," I said to Marsh and he nodded.

"Very attractive. Last night, when I walked along it the crickets were buzzing in the trees." They weren't crickets, of course, but I didn't correct the man from Chicago. "A lot of living-room lights were lighted, and now and then I heard voices murmuring from front porches. There were fireflies over the lawns and bushes, and all in all I walked a lot farther than I'd meant to. So when I saw a streetcar coming toward me I decided I'd ride back to Main Street." Marsh leaned toward me, his cigar between thumb and forefinger, pointing its butt end at me. "You hear what I say? I said I saw that streetcar and I heard it, too, I don't care what anyone tells you." He sat back in his chair, regarding me bitterly, then continued.

"It was still a long way off when I first noticed it. But I saw the single round headlight moving slowly along toward me, swaying above the track down the middle of the street. Then I saw the light begin to glint along the rails, and a moment later heard the sound—there's no other sound just like it; a sort of steady, metallic hiss—of a streetcar moving along the rails.

"I saw it, I heard it, and I stepped out into the street to wait for it; there was no other traffic. I just stood there in the middle of the street beside the track waiting and thinking absently about the new factory. Down the street somewhere a phonograph was playing. I recognized the tune; it was 'Wabash Blues,' and it slowed down for a few moments, the notes growling as they got slower and deeper. Then someone wound the phonograph and it speeded right up.

"Now, that motorman saw me; he must have. I signaled to make sure as the car came closer, stepping right up beside the rails to get into the beam of its light, and waving one arm. So he saw me, all right, and I saw him, very plainly. He had on a black uniform cap and wore a large mustache. He had on a blue shirt with a white stiff collar and a black tie, and a vest with flat metal buttons, and a gold watch chain stretching from pocket to pocket. That's how close I saw him but he never so much as glanced at me. I stood right there in the beam of his light waving my arm; it made a big swaying shadow down the street past us. Then all of a sudden, that car right on top of me, I saw that he wasn't going to stop; he hadn't even slowed down.

"The car swelled out at the sides the way a streetcar does,

protruding well past the rails, and I was right next to the tracks. I was about to be hit by that car, I suddenly realized; *would* have been hit if I hadn't dropped back, falling to the street behind me like a ballplayer at bat dropping away from a badly pitched ball. Right back and down on my haunches I went, then lost my balance and sprawled out flat on my back on the street as that car rocked past me straight through the space I'd been standing in and went on by like a little island of light swaying off down the rails.

"I yelled after it. I was badly scared and I cursed that guy out. Still lying on my back in the dust of the street, I shouted so he could hear me, and a porch light snapped on. I didn't care; I was mad. Getting to my feet, I yelled after that guy some more, watching him shrink and disappear down the rails, his trolley sparking blue every once in a while, as though it were answering me. More porch lights were coming on now, and several men in shirt sleeves from the houses up beyond the lawns came walking toward me. I heard their feet scuffle as they crossed the walks.

"Well, I expect I was a sight, all right, standing in the middle of the street shouting and shaking my fist after that streetcar, the entire back of my suit covered with dust, my hat in the gutter somewhere. They asked me, those men, stopping around me—speaking pleasantly and politely enough—what the trouble was. I could see women and children standing on porch steps, watching. I answered. I told them how that streetcar had nearly run me down. This might not be a regular stop, I said; I didn't know about that. But that was no excuse to run a man down without even clanging his bell to warn me. No reason he couldn't have stopped, anyway; there were no other passengers, no reason to be in such a hurry. They agreed with me, helping me find my hat, dusting me off. I expect it was one of the women who phoned the police—one of the men signaling to her behind my back, probably. Anyway, they got there pretty quickly and quietly. It wasn't till I heard the car door slam behind me that I turned and saw the police car, a sixty-two Plymouth with white doors, the two cops already out in the street and walking toward me.

"'Drunk and disorderly,' or something of the sort, was the charge they arrested me on. I argued, I protested; I wasn't drunk. But one of the cops just said, 'Show me the streetcar tracks, mister; just point them out and we'll let you go.'" Marsh looked at me, his face set and angry. "And of course there aren't any tracks. There haven't been any on Broad Street since—"

"Since they tore them up sometime in the thirties," I said. "I know."

Marsh was nodding. "So of course you don't believe me, either. Well, I don't blame you. No one else did; why should you? I had to phone one of the councilmen to come down to the jail and identify me, and, when he arrived, he had the attorney from the city with him. They vouched for me, and apologized, and got me out of jail, and kept their faces straight. Too straight; I knew they were laughing inside, and that it's a story I could never live down here, never at all. So I'm leaving Galesburg. There are plenty of other towns along the Santa Fe to build a factory in."

"I didn't say I didn't believe you." I leaned toward him and spoke quietly. "Tell me something. How big was that streetcar?"

Marsh squinted at the ceiling. "Small," he said then, his voice a little surprised. "Very small, actually; wouldn't hold much more than a dozen people or so."

I nodded, still leaning over the tabletop. "You saw the motorman up close, you said, and it was a warm night. Did you happen to notice his cap? What was his cap like, besides being black?"

Marsh thought again, then smiled. "I'll be darned," he said. "Yes, I remember; it was wicker. It was a regular uniform cap, just like any other in shape, and with a shiny peak and a stiff hard top. But the top was made of wicker—actual wickerwork—dyed black. I never saw a cap like that before in my life."

"Neither did I; nowhere else but here. But that's the kind of cap streetcar motormen used to wear in the summer in Galesburg, Illinois. I was just a little kid but I remember them. What color was that streetcar, red or green?"

"It was yellow," Marsh said quietly. "I saw it pass under a street light just before it reached me, and it was yellow."

"That's right," I said. "The streetcars in Galesburg were painted yellow, and the last of them quit running years ago." I stood up and put my knuckles on the tabletop, resting my weight on them, leaning down to look Marsh in the eyes. "But you saw one last night just the same. I don't know how or why but you did, and I know it and believe you." I smiled, straightening up to stand beside the table. "But no one else ever will. Of course you're right; you'd never enjoy living in Galesburg now."

Do you see what I mean? Do you see why I'm a reporter? How else would you hear a story like that at first hand? I never turned it in, of course; I just wrote that Mr. E. V. Marsh, of Chicago, had considered but decided against building a factory here, and it ran as a little five-inch story on page three. But it's because of occasional stories like Marsh's that I expect to continue reporting for the *Register-Mail* as long as I live or can get around. I know the town laughs at me a little for that; it's been a long time since Galesburg took me seriously, though it once expected big things of me.

I was first in my high-school class, in fact, and was offered a scholarship at Harvard. But I didn't take it. I went to Knox, the local college right here in town, working my way through —my mother was alive then but my father was dead and we didn't have much money. That's when I started reporting for the *Register-Mail,* full time in the summers, part time during school, and I graduated second in my class, Phi Beta Kappa, *summa cum laude,* and could have had any of several scholarships for postgrad work, or a job with American Chicle in South America. The town thought I was going places, and so did a girl I was engaged to—a junior at Knox, from Chicago. But I wasn't going anywhere and knew it; and I turned down every offer that would take me from Galesburg, and when she graduated next year the girl turned me down and went home.

So there's my trouble, if trouble it is; I'm in love with a town, in love with the handful of Main Street buildings that were built in the last century and that don't look much different, except for the modernized store fronts, from the way they do in the old photographs. Look at their upper stories, as I always do walking along Main, at the tall slim windows with the rounded tops, and maybe, just maybe, you're seeing at least one of the buildings Abraham Lincoln saw when he was in Galesburg. Yes; he debated Douglas on a wooden platform built over the east steps of Old Main at Knox, something the college never seems to get tired of reminding the world about. And Old Main, too, stands very little changed, on the outside, anyway, from the day Lincoln stood there grasping his coat lapels and smiling down at Douglas.

There's sordidness and desolation in Galesburg, and just plain ugliness, too. But in so many other places and ways it's a fine old town, and I move through its streets, buildings, and private houses every day of my life, and know more about

Galesburg in many ways than anyone else, I'm certain. I know that E. V. Marsh really saw the streetcar he said he did, whether that's possible or not; and I know why the old Pollard place out on Fremont Street didn't burn down.

The morning after the fire I was driving by on my way to work and saw Doug Blaisdel standing in the side yard, waist deep in yellow weeds. I thought he'd finally sold the place—he's the real-estate man who was handling it—and I pulled in to the curb to see who'd bought it. Then, turning off the ignition, I saw that wasn't it because Doug was standing, fists on his hips, staring up at the side of the building, and now I noticed half a dozen kids there, too, and knew that something had happened.

Doug saw me stop, and as I opened the front gate he turned from the old building to cut across the front yard through the weeds to meet me. The place is on a great big lot, and there's a wrought-iron fence, rusting but in good shape, that runs across the lot in front by the sidewalk. A small gate opens onto a walk leading to the porch, and a larger taller pair of gates opens onto what was once a carriage drive to a portico at the west side of the house. Closing the small gate behind me, I was looking up at the house admiring it as always; it looks like an only slightly smaller Mount Vernon, with four great two-story pillars rising to the roof from a ground-level brick-paved porch, and there's an enormous fanlight above the double front doors. But the old place was at least five years overdue for painting; the heirs live in California and have never even seen it, so it sat empty and they didn't keep it up.

"What's the trouble?" I called to Doug when I got close enough.

He's a brisk, young, heavy-rimmed-glasses type from Chicago; been here about five years. "Fire," he said, and beckoned with his chin to follow, turning back across the yard toward the house, the kids trooping along.

At the side of the house I stood looking up at the damage. The fire had obviously started inside, bursting out a window, and now the white clapboard outside wall was scorched and charred clear to the roof, the upper part of the window frame ruined. Stepping to the window to lean inside the house, I saw there wasn't much damage there. It looked as though the dining-room wallpaper, peeling and hanging loose, had somehow caught fire; but outside of soot stains the heavy plaster wall didn't seem much damaged. Mostly it was the window frame, both inside and out, that had burned; that was all. But it was ruined and would cost several hundred dollars to replace.

I said so to Doug, and he nodded and said, "A lot more than the owners will ever spend. They'll just tell me to have the opening boarded over. Too bad the place didn't burn right down."

"Oh?" I said.

He nodded again, shrugging. "Sure. It's a white elephant, Oscar; you know that. Twenty-four rooms, including a ballroom. Who wants it? Been empty eight years now and there's never been a real prospect for it. Cost plenty to fix it up right, and just about as much to tear it down. Burned to the ground, though"—his brows rose at the thought—"the site empty, I could sell the lot for an apartment building if I could get it rezoned, and I probably could." He grinned at me; everybody likes Doug Blaisdel; he insists on it. "But don't worry," he said. "I didn't start the fire. If I had, I'd have done a better job."

He glanced up at the blackened strip of wall again, then down at the ground around us, and I looked, too. We were standing on what had been the old graveled carriage drive, though the white gravel had long since washed away and it was just dirt now; it was trampled and soggy.

"Somebody put the fire out," Doug said, nodding at the damp ground, "but I can't find out who. Wasn't the fire department; they never got a call and don't know a thing about it. Neither do any of the neighbors. Nobody seems to have seen it."

"I heard the fire bell," one of the kids said. "It woke me up, but then I fell asleep again."

"You did not! You're crazy! You were dreamin'!" another boy answered, and they began wrestling, not serious but laughing.

Doug turned toward the street. "Well, back to work!" he said brightly. "See you around, Oscar. You going to put this in the paper?"

I glanced up at the house again and shrugged. "I don't know; not much of a story. We'll see."

The kids left, too, chasing each other through the weeds, horsing around, no longer interested; but I stood in the old driveway beside the house for a few moments longer. Old Man Nordstrum, as he's been called since he was thirty, I guess, lived in the house next door; and whoever had put this fire out, he'd heard it and seen it, maybe done it himself, no matter what he'd told Doug Blaisdel. I looked over suddenly at the side windows of his place, and he was standing watching me. When he saw that I'd seen him, he grinned. Doug was in his car now, the motor started; he flicked a hand at me, then glanced over his shoulder at the street, and pulled out. Smiling a little, I beckoned Nordstrum to come out.

He came out his front door, buttoning an old tan-and-brown sweater, walked to his front gate, then turned into the old Pollard driveway toward me. He's about seventy-one, a retired lawyer with a reputation for grouchiness. But it's less grouchiness, I think, than a simple unwillingness to put up with anyone who doesn't interest him. He's rich, one of the best lawyers in the state; he's bald and has a lined face with smart brown eyes; a shrewd man.

"Doug Blasidel tells me you didn't see the fire last night," I said as he walked toward me.

Nordstrum shook his head. "Blaisdel is inaccurate, as usual; that's only what I told him. I saw it; of course I saw it. How could I sleep through a fire right outside my bedroom window?"

"Why didn't you tell Doug about it, Mr. Nordstrum?"

"Because he's a fool. Has it all figured out what he's going to believe for the rest of his life; it takes a fool to do that. But I don't think you're a fool, Oscar, not that kind, so I'll tell you; glad to tell somebody. What wakened me—this was at just three-fourteen this morning; I looked at my luminous alarm clock—was a sound." Eyes narrowing, choosing his words carefully, he said, "It was a combined sound—the crackle of growing flames and just the touch of a clapper on a brass fire gong. I opened my eyes, saw the orange light of flames reflected from my bedroom walls, and I jumped out of bed and grabbed my glasses. I looked out my window and saw the fire next door here, the flames and sparks shooting out the window in a strong updraft, licking the eaves two stories up; and I saw the fire engine a dozen yards away toward the street, and the firemen were tugging at the hose, unreeling it just as fast as they could pull. I stood and watched them. Best view of a fire I ever had.

"They worked fast; they got their hose connected to the hydrant out at the curb, and they had a good stream on the fire, the pumper at work, in no more than a minute. In five minutes, maybe less, they had the fire completely out and wet down good. Then they packed up their hose and left."

Nordstrum stood there in his old-style button sweater, looking at me over the top of his glasses.

"Well, what's so hard to believe about that?" I asked.

"The fire engine, Oscar, had a tall, upright, cylindrical boiler made of polished brass, narrowing at the top to a short smokestack. It looked like a boy's steam engine, only a thousand times larger. Underneath that boiler was a fire made of wood and coal; that's what heated the water that supplied steam pressure for the pump. The whole thing, my boy, along with hose, axes, and all the rest of it, was mounted on a low-slung wagon body with big wooden spoke wheels, painted red; and it was pulled by four big gray horses who stood waiting in the light of the fire stomping their hoofs in the soft dirt now and then and switching their tails.

"And when the fire was out and the hose reloaded, the firemen climbed onto the fire engine—two in the high seat up front, where the reins were; the others on the low step in back, hanging on—and the horses pulled it down the driveway, turned onto Fremont Street, breaking into a trot, and that's the last I could see of them. The firemen wore helmets and rubber coats, and they all had large mustaches, and one had a beard. Now, what about it, Oscar? You think I don't know what I saw?"

I shook my head. "Hard to see how you could be mistaken about what you saw unless you've suddenly gone crazy."

"Which I have not," said Nordstrum. "Not yet. Come here." He turned to walk down the old carriageway toward the street, then stopped and pointed. "Here's where the horses stood," he said, "well away from the heat of the fire."

I looked down at the dirt and saw the horseshoe marks sharp and plain in the damp black earth, dozens of them, overlapping. Nordstrum pointed again with his foot and I saw the manure and, deeply imprinted in the earth at the edges of the carriageway, the long indented ribbons that were wagon tracks.

That was just under a year ago. Two months later, in September, Doug Blaisdel sold the Pollard place—cheap, as he had to, but still he was glad now that it hadn't burned down—to a retired farm-equipment dealer from Peoria who'd grown up in Galesburg. It took all last winter and I don't know how much money—the farm-equipment business must have been good—to get the old place fixed up; but now it looks the way it always used to, clean and white again, the lawn and iron fence and the burned window restored, and the inside of the house is beautiful. They've got an unmarried daughter, and last Friday they gave a dance in the old ballroom. It was a big affair, and walking up the path to the house—the daughter had invited me—I saw the house all lighted up, heard the music, and saw all the people at the windows and out on the huge porch, the big old house white and fresh and alive again, and I was glad it hadn't burned down and the site sold for an apartment building.

Do you see? Do you understand now what's happening in Galesburg? If you do, then you know why the phone rang late one night last fall out at the old Denigmann farm. It's one of the finest of the farms just past the city limits; a wonderful place. There are a half-dozen acres of fine woodland including some nut trees; there's a small but deep stream that winds through the whole farm and is wide enough for swimming in several places; and scattered over two acres of corn land are a dozen regularly shaped mounds which the kids out there have always believed were Indian burial mounds, and around which every generation of Denigmanns since they've owned the place has carefully plowed.

A lot of the neighboring farms are gone without a trace, the land covered with new houses. That's necessary, of course, and some of them are nice ones. But you wonder why so many of the houses we build nowadays are so tiny, so lightly built, and so nearly identical. And why it's necessary to lay them out in indistinguishable rows alongside raw concrete streets without even sidewalks for children to play on. And why they've simply got to be jammed together a few feet apart, on what was once Illinois prairie with an unlimited horizon. Can you imagine some of the houses we build today lived in and loved a century from now?

Carl Denigmann was going to sell his place to the subdividers, too, a big Florida outfit that was reaching up into the North. It was a good offer; he was fifty-nine years old, a widower, his children all grown and gone; why not? Late one night, he told me—this was last November, about the middle of the month, after all his crops were in—he was sitting alone in the farm kitchen thinking about it. Carl's a small, strong man with black heavily grayed hair, all of which he still has, and he was probably smoking a pipe there in the farm kitchen.

Now, the Galesburg telephone company is an independent, and in the fall of last year it brought various country phone lines up to date including Denigmann's—putting lines underground and installing dial phones. And in many a place, Carl's included, the company didn't bother removing the old out-of-date and now useless wall phone, unless the customer insisted on getting rid of it.

So Carl sat in his kitchen—there's a ninety-year-old fireplace in it, and he had a fire going—staring at the fire and thinking, smoking his pipe, I'm sure. And when the telephone rang—the stuttering, uncertain grumbling ring of an old hand-crank phone—he simply got up, stepped to the wall, and answered it as he'd done hundreds of times all through his life. The conversation, then, was ordinary enough; it was just Billy Amling asking Carl if he wanted to go rabbit hunting with their twenty-twos in the woods after school next day, keeping one eye open, as usual, for arrowheads. Carl listened, half nodding, ready to agree, as always, before it came back into his head that Billy had been killed in the war in France in 1918; and the telephone receiver lay dead in his hand, not in the way of a phone when the other party has hung up, but in the completely lifeless way of a telephone that is connected to nothing any more and is just hanging on a wall without even wires leading away to the outside now.

Nearly all the rest of the night Carl Denigmann sat up thinking of all the farm had been to him, and Billy Amling, and many others, including Denigmanns who were dead long before he'd been born. And this spring Carl is out plowing it again and he expects to keep farming for at least a few more years. By then, he told me, he'll have figured out what to do; he thinks maybe Galesburg might accept the old farm as a sort of park or preserve, with picnic tables, maybe, but mostly leaving it pretty much as is for kids to hunt through with their twenty-twos, and swim in the creek, and prowl around the old mounds, and pretend, at least, that they're Indian graves. Carl doesn't know, exactly, what he'll do about the farm; he just knows he's not going to let them subdivide it.

I'm glad about that; just as I'm glad the old Pollard place was saved, and that there won't be a great big factory right out at the end of Broad Street, and about a lot of other things I haven't got time to tell. I'm glad because here in Galesburg, and everywhere else, of course, they're trying—endlessly—to destroy the beauty we inherit from the past. They keep trying, and when they succeed, they replace it—not always, but all too often—with drabness and worse. With a sterile sun-baked parking lot where decrepit, characterful, old Boone's Alley once ran; rechristening the asphalt-paved nothingness (as though even the memory of old Boone's Alley must be blotted from mind) with the characterless title Park Plaza. And with anonymous apartment buildings where fine old houses once stood. With concrete-block ugliness sprawling along what were charming country roads. With—but you know what they're doing; wherever you live, you see it all around you. They even want to level Galesburg's ancient Public Square into—well, a parking lot, of course, as though there were nothing more important.

And who are "they?" Why, "they" are us, of course; who else? We're doing these things to ourselves as though we were powerless to stop; or as though any feeling for beauty or grace or a sense of the past were a kind of sentimental weakness to be jeered down. So what has been happening in Galesburg? Why, it's simple enough.

Galesburg's past is fighting back. It's *resisting* us, for the past isn't so easily destroyed; it's not simply gone with yesterday's newspaper. No, it is not, for it has been far too much—we are all products of it—to ever be completely gone. And so, somehow, in Galesburg, Illinois, when it's been necessary as it sometimes has, the past has fought against the present. When the need becomes desperate enough, then the old yellow streetcars, or horse-drawn fire engines, or abandoned wall phones can and do flicker into momentary existence again, struggling to keep what I and so many others—Carl Sandburg, for one, who was born here—love about Galesburg, Illinois.

It's hard to say whether it's succeeding; they did, after all, chop down a lot of fine old Galesburg elms to widen Losey Street; Boone's Alley is gone; and last year the library burned down and the townspeople voted against rebuilding it. And yet—well, I'd hate to be responsible for turning the old square into a parking lot, I can tell you that much. Because just last night, for example, I learned that those twenty-odd old elm trees on that big corner lot on north Cedar Street will not, after all, be chopped down. The man who was going to whack down with a power saw these trees older than himself—he was tired of raking leaves every fall, he said—is in the hospital instead, with a broken leg in traction. It's strung up in a wire-and-pulley contraption like a broken leg in a comic strip. The neighbor who saw what happened told me that the man was standing out in the street last night looking up at the old trees and estimating which way they'd fall when he sliced through them this weekend. All of a sudden he was struck by a car that appeared out of nowhere. The police report calls it a hit-and-run accident, which it was, and the chief has assured the *Register-Mail* that they'll find the car very soon. It shouldn't be hard to find, they feel, because the neighbor who saw it happen got a good look at the car and furnished a complete description. It was a 1916 Buick roadster with a red body, varnished spoke wheels, and big polished brass headlights each the size of a small drum.

Such Interesting Neighbors

I can't honestly say I knew from the start that there was something queer about the Hellenbeks. I did notice some strange things right away, and wondered about them, but I shrugged them off. They were nice people; I liked them; and everyone has a few odd little tricks.

We were watching from our sun-parlor windows the day they arrived; not snooping or prying, you understand, but naturally we were curious. Nell and I are pretty sociable and we were hoping a couple around our own ages would move into the new house next door.

I was just finishing breakfast—it was a Saturday and I wasn't working—and Nell was running the vacuum cleaner over the sun-parlor rug. I heard the vacuum shut off, and Nell called out, "Here they are, Al!" and I ran in and we got our first look at the Hellenbeks.

He was helping her from a cab, and I got a good look at him and his wife. They seemed to be just about our ages, the man maybe thirty-two or so and his wife in her middle twenties. She was rather pretty, and he had a nice, agreeable kind of face.

"Newlyweds?" Nell said, a little excited.

"Why?"

"Their clothes are all brand-new. Even the shoes. And so's the bag."

"Yeah, maybe you're right." I watched for a second or so, then said, "Foreigners, too, I think," showing Nell I was pretty observant myself.

"Why do you think so?"

"He's having trouble with the local currency." He was, too. He couldn't seem to pick out the right change, and finally he held out his hand and let the driver find the right coins.

But we were wrong on both counts. They'd been married three years, we found out later, had both been born in the States, and had lived here nearly all their lives.

Furniture deliveries began arriving next door within half an hour; everything new, all bought from local merchants. We live in San Rafael, California, in a neighborhood of small houses. Mostly young people live here, and it's a friendly, informal place. So after a while I got into an old pair of flannels and sneakers and wandered over to get acquainted and lend a hand if I could, and I cut across the two lawns. As I came up to their house, I heard them talking in the living room. "Here's a picture of Truman," he said, and I heard a newspaper rattle.

"Truman," she said, kind of thoughtfully. "Let's see now; doesn't Roosevelt come next?"

"No, Truman comes *after* Roosevelt."

"I think you're wrong, dear," she said. "It's Truman, then Roosevelt, then—"

When my feet hit their front steps, the talk stopped. At the door I knocked and glanced in; they were sitting on the living-room floor, and Ted Hellenbek was just scrambling to his feet. They'd been unpacking a carton of dishes and there was a bunch of wadded-up old newspapers lying around, and I guess they'd been looking at those. Ted came to the door. He'd changed to a T-shirt, slacks and moccasins, all brand-new.

"I'm Al Lewis from next door," I said. "Thought maybe I could give you a hand."

"Glad to know you." He pushed the door open, then stuck out his hand. "I'm Ted Hellenbek," and he grinned in a nice friendly way. His wife got up from the floor, and Ted introduced us. Her name was Ann.

Well, I worked around with them the rest of the morning, helping them unpack things, and we got the place into pretty good order. While we were working, Ted told me they'd been living in South America—he didn't say where or why—and that they'd sold everything they had down there, except the clothes they traveled in and a few personal belongings, rather than pay shipping expenses. That sounded perfectly reasonable and sensible, except that a few days later Ann told Nell their house in South America had burned down and they'd lost everything.

Maybe half an hour after I arrived, some bedding was delivered—blankets, pillows, linen, stuff like that. Ann picked up the two pillows, put cases on them, and turned toward the bedroom. Now, it was broad daylight, the bedroom door was closed, and it was made of solid wood. But Ann walked straight into that door and fell. I couldn't figure out how she came to do it; it was as though she expected the door to open by itself or something. That's what Ted said, too, going over to help her up. "Be careful, honey," he said, and laughed a little, making a joke of it. "You'll have to learn, you know, that doors won't open themselves."

Around eleven thirty or so, some books arrived, quite a slew of them, and all new. We were squatting on the floor, unpacking them, and Ted picked up a book, showed me the title, and said, "Have you read this?"

It was "The Far Reaches," by a Walter Braden. "No," I said. "I read the reviews a week or so ago, and they weren't so hot."

"I know," Ted said, and he had a funny smile on his face. "And yet it's a great book. Just think," he went on, and shook his head a little, "you can buy this now, a new copy, first edition, for three dollars. Yet in—oh, a hundred and forty years, say, a copy like this might be worth five to eight thousand dollars."

"Could be," I said, and shrugged; but what kind of a remark is that? Sure, any book you want to name might be valuable someday, but why *that* book? And why a hundred and forty years? And why five to eight thousand dollars, particularly? Well, that's the kind of thing I mean about the Hellenbeks. It wasn't that anything big or dramatic or really out of the way happened that first day. It was just that every once in a while one or the other would do or say something that wasn't quite right.

Most of the time, though, things were perfectly ordinary and normal. We talked and laughed and kidded around a lot, and I knew I was going to like the Hellenbeks and that Nelly would, too.

In the afternoon we got pretty hot and thirsty, so I went home and brought back some beer. This time Nelly came with me, met the new people, and invited them over for supper. Nelly complimented Ann on the nice things she had, and Ann thanked her and apologized, the way a woman will, because things were kind of dusty. Then she went out to the kitchen, came back with a dustcloth, and started dusting around. It was a white cloth with a small green pattern, and it got pretty dirty, and when she wiped off the window sills it was really streaked.

Then Ann leaned out the front window, shook the cloth once, and—it was clean again. I mean *completely* clean; the dirt, every trace of it, shook right out. She did that several times, dusting around the room and then shaking the cloth out, and it shook out white every time.

Well, Nelly sat there with her mouth hanging open, and finally she said, "Where in the world did you get that dust-cloth?"

Ann glanced down at the cloth in her hand, then looked up at Nelly again and said, "Why, it's just an old rag, from one of Ted's old suits." Then suddenly she blushed.

I'd have blushed, too; did you ever see a man's suit, white with a little green pattern?

Nell said, "Well, I never saw a dustcloth before that would shake out perfectly clean. Mine certainly don't."

Ann turned even redder, looking absolutely confused, and—I'd say *scared*. She mumbled something about cloth in South America, glanced at Ted, and then put the back of her wrist up against her forehead, and for an instant I'd have sworn she was going to cry.

But Ted got up fast, put his arm around Ann's waist and turned her a little so her back was toward us, and said something about how she'd been working too hard and was tired. His eyes, though, as he stood looking at us over Ann's shoulder, were hard and defiant. For a moment you almost got the feeling that it was the two of them against the world, that Ted was protecting Ann against us.

Then Nelly ran a hand admiringly over the top of the end table beside her and said how much she liked it, and Ann turned and smiled and thanked her. Nelly got up and led

Ann off to the bedroom, telling her not to try to do too much all in one day, and when they came out a little later everything was all right.

We got to know the Hellenbeks pretty well. They were casual, easygoing, and always good company. In no time Nelly and Ann were doing their marketing together, dropping in on each other during the day, and trading recipes.

At night, out watering our lawns or cutting the grass or something, Ted and I would usually bat the breeze about one thing or another till it got dark. We talked politics, high prices, gardening, stuff like that. He knew plenty about politics and world events, and it was surprising the way his predictions would turn out. At first I offered to bet with him about a few things we disagreed about, but he never would and I'm glad he didn't; he was seldom wrong when it came to guessing what was going to happen.

Well, that's the way things were. We'd drop in on each other, take Sunday drives together and go on picnics, play a little bridge at night and on week ends.

Odd little things would still happen occasionally, but less and less often as time went by—and none of them were ever repeated. When Ted bought something now, he never had trouble finding the right change, and he didn't discover any more rare old new books, and Ann stopped walking into doors.

They were always interesting neighbors, though. For one thing, Ted was an inventor. I don't know why that should have surprised me, but it did. There are such things as inventors; they have to live somewhere, and there's no good reason why one shouldn't move in next door to us. But Ted didn't *seem* like an inventor; why, the first time he cut their grass, I had to show him how to adjust the set screw that keeps the blades in alignment.

But just the same he was an inventor and a good one. One evening I was picking tomatoes in the little garden we have, and Ted wandered over, tossing something into the air and catching it again. I thought it was a paper clip at first. Ted stood watching me for a minute or so, and then he squatted down beside me and held out this thing in his hand and said, "Ever see anything like this before?"

I took it and looked at it; it was a piece of thin wire bent at each end to form two egg-shaped loops. Then the wire had been bent again at the middle so that the two loops slid together. I can't explain it very well, but I could make you one easy in half a minute. "What is it?" I said, and handed it back to him.

"A little invention—the Saf-T-Clip," he said. "You use it wherever you'd ordinarily use a safety pin. Here." He unbuttoned one of my shirt buttons and slid the thing onto the two layers of cloth.

Well, do you know that I couldn't unfasten my shirt where that little thing gripped it? Even when I took hold of both sides of my shirt and pulled, that little piece of twisted wire just dug in and held. Yet when Ted showed me how to undo it—you just pressed the wire at a certain place—it slid right off. It was just the kind of simple thing you wonder, "Now, why didn't somebody ever think of that before?"

I told Ted I thought it was a hell of a good idea. "How'd you happen to think of it?" I asked.

He smiled. "Oh, it was surprisingly easy. That's how I'm planning to make a living, Al—inventing little things. First thing I did, the day we arrived in San Rafael, was get a patent application sent off on this thing. Then I mailed a sample to a wire company." He grinned happily and said, "I got a reply today; they'll buy it outright for fifteen hundred dollars."

"You going to take it?"

"Sure. I don't think it's the best offer in the world and I might do better if I shopped around. But I've been a little worried, frankly, about how we were going to pay for the furniture and stuff we bought, and the house rent." He shrugged. "So I'm glad to get this money. We'll be okay, now, till I finish the next project."

"What's the next one?" I said. "If you can tell me, that is." I set the tomatoes down and sat down on the grass.

"Sure, I can tell you," he said. "Picture a flashlight with a little dial set in just above the button. There's a lens, but it curves inward, and it's painted black except for a tiny round hole in the center. Press the button and a little beam of light—a special *kind* of light—no thicker than a pencil lead, shoots out. The beam doesn't spread, either; it stays the same thickness. You get the idea?"

"Yeah. What's it for?"

"For measuring distances. Turn it on, aim the little dot of light so it hits the end of any distance you want to measure. Then look at the dial, and you can read off the distance from the dot of light to the edge of the lens in feet and fractions of an inch, down to sixteenths." He smiled. "Sound good?"

"Hell, yes," I said. "But how will it work?"

"On flashlight batteries," Ted said, and stood up, as if that were an answer.

Well, I took the hint and didn't ask any more questions, but if he can make a thing like that—a guy who had to have help adjusting his lawn mower—then I'll eat it when he's finished. And yet, darned if I don't think, sometimes, that he might do it at that.

Oh, Hellenbek's an interesting guy, all right. Told me once that in fifty years they'd be growing full-grown trees from seeds in ten days' time. Indoors, too, and with absolutely straight grain and no knots; regular wood factories. I asked him what made him think so and he shrugged and said it was just an idea he had. But you see what I mean; the Hellenbeks were interesting neighbors.

I guess the most interesting time we ever spent with them, though, was one evening on our front porch. Supper was over, and I was reading a magazine that had come in the mail that morning. Nell was on the porch swing, knitting. The magazine I was reading was all science fiction—trips to Mars in space ships, gun fights with atomic pistols, and so on. I get a kick out of that kind of stuff, though Nell thinks it's silly.

Pretty soon the Hellenbeks wandered over. Ann sat down with Nelly, and Ted leaned on the porch rail, facing my chair. "What're you reading?" he said, nodding at the magazine in my lap.

I handed it to him, a little embarrassed. The cover illustration showed a man from Jupiter with eyes on the ends of long tentacles. "Don't know if you ever read this kind of stuff or not," I said.

Ann said to Nell, "I tried that biscuit mix. It's wonderful."

"Oh, did you like it?" Nell was pleased, and they started talking food and cooking.

Ted began leafing through my magazine, and I lighted a cigarette and just sat there looking out at the street, feeling lazy and comfortable. It was a nice night, and still pretty light out. Ted got very quiet, slowly turning the pages, studying the illustrations, reading a paragraph or so here and there, and once he said, "Well, I'll be damned," sort of half under his breath.

He must have looked through that magazine for ten minutes or more, and I could tell he was fascinated. Finally he looked up, handed the magazine back, and said, kind of surprised, "That's very interesting, really very interesting."

"Yeah, some of the science-fiction stuff is pretty good," I

said. "There was a magazine story not long ago, by Ray Bradbury. About a man of the future who escapes back to our times. But then the secret police of the future come for him and take him back."

"Really?" Ted said. "I missed that."

"It might be around the house. If I find it, I'll give it to you."

"I'd like to see it," he said. I had the impression that that sort of thing was brand-new to Ted, but I was wrong because then he said, "Now that I know you're interested——" For just a moment he hesitated; then he went on, "Well, the fact is I wrote a science-fiction story myself once."

Ann glanced up quickly, the way a woman does when her husband gets off on the wrong subject. Then she turned back to Nell, smiling and nodding, but I could tell she was listening to Ted.

"Yeah?" I said.

"Yeah. I worked out this story on the world of the future that you——"

"Ted!" said Ann.

But he just grinned at her and went on talking to me. "Ann's always afraid I'll bore people with some of my ideas."

"Well, this one's *silly,*" Ann said.

"Of course it is," Nell said, soothing her down. "I can't understand why Al reads that sort of thing."

"Well, you just go on with your talk, then," Ted said. "You don't have to listen. Honey," he said to Ann, "this is different; this is all right."

"Sure," I said, "it's harmless. At least we're not out drinking or hanging around the pool hall."

"Well . . ." He shifted his position and was smiling, very eager, almost excited. I could tell this was something he was itching to talk about. "A friend of mine and I used to talk a little about this kind of stuff, and we worked out a story.

Matter of fact, we did more than that. He was an amateur printer; had his own printing press in the basement. Did beautiful work. So one time, just for a gag, we printed up an article, a magazine, the way it might look and read sometime in the future. I've still got a copy or two around somewhere. Like to see it?"

"Ted," Ann said pleadingly.

"It's all *right,* Honey," he said.

Well, of course I said sure, I'd like to see his article, and Ted went on over to their house and in a minute or so he came back with a long narrow strip of paper and handed it to me.

It didn't feel like paper when I took it; it was almost like fine linen to the touch, and it didn't rattle or crackle, but it was stiff like paper. At the top of the page, there was a title, printed in red—long thin letters, but very easy to read. It said: TIME ON OUR HANDS? Underneath was a caption: *Should TT be outlawed? A grave new question facing a world already stunned with fear of oxygen-reversion, population-deterrent and "crazy-molecule" weapons.*

Ted said, "The funny shape of the page is because that's how it comes out of the teleprint receivers in subscribers' homes."

Both the women looked at him contemptuously, and went on with their conversation.

"Pretty elaborate gag," I said.

"I know," he said, and laughed. "We spent a lot of time fooling around with that thing."

I turned back to the article, and a picture in the middle of the page caught my eye. It was a man's face, smiling, and it seemed to stick right out of the page. It was taken full face, yet you could see the nose jutting out at you, and the ears and sides of the head seemed farther back in the page. It was beautifully printed and in marvelous color. You could see fine lines around the eyes, the film of moisture on the eyeballs, and every separate strand of hair. I raised the picture closer to my eyes and it went flat, two-dimensional, and I could see it was printed, all right. But when I lowered it to reading distance again, the photograph popped out in three dimensions once more, a perfect miniature human face.

The caption said: *Ralph Kent, thirty-two-year-old quantum physicist and world's first Time-Traveler. His initial words upon his reappearance in the laboratory after testing TT are now world-famous. "Nobody in sixteenth-century England," he announced, "seems to understand English."*

"Your friend does some pretty fine printing," I said to Ted.

"The photograph?" he said. "Oh, you can get results like that if you're willing to take the time. Go ahead; read the article."

I lighted another cigarette and started to read. The article said:

The first practical Time-machine reached blue-print stage in the Schenectady laboratories of the De-Farday Electric Company in November of last year, a closely guarded secret among seven top officials of the company. It is said to have been based on an extension of the basic theories of Albert Einstein, famous theoretical physicist of the last century.

A handmade pilot model of DE's astounding invention was completed on May 18th of this year at a cost, excluding four years' preliminary research expense, of approximately $190,000. *But even before it was completed and successfully tested, it was out of date. A young Australian physicist, Finis Bride, of the University of Melbourne, had published accounts of experiments in which he had successfully substituted a cheaply maintained electric flow-field for the conventional and expensive platinum-alloy heretofore used in gravity-repulsion. The way was cleared, as DE officials were quick to realize, for inexpensive mass production of Time-machines.*

It was vitally important, DE's board decided, to try to keep the young Australian's invention a secret from competitors. But almost inevitably, while DE was in the process of tooling up, the secret leaked, and soon Asco, BCA and Eastern Electric were in the race to hit the market first. Almost as quickly, British, French, Russian, Italian, and, soon after, televip manufacturers throughout the entire world were in the scramble. By June of this year TT sets were selling at the rate . . .

Ted's article went on like that. It was really cleverly done. There were times when you'd almost think you were reading the real McCoy. It told how Time-Travel sets hit the market with a big advertising splash early in the summer. The first day they went on sale the public was apathetic and skeptical. But the following day the press and the televip networks (whatever they were supposed to be) were filled with interviews with people who'd tried Time-Travel, and they were all absolutely bug-eyed with astonishment because the damned machine actually worked.

You put a little gadget in your pocket called a "tampered relay." Then you turned on your set, adjusted the dials, stepped into a little beam of invisible light, and you'd appear instantly at just about any time and place you'd set the dials for. You left the set on, or adjusted it to turn on automatically after a certain length of time, and as long as you still had your "tampered relay" all you had to do was stand in the same spot you'd first appeared in and you'd be right back home again standing in the beam of invisible light. Well, the public went nuts for it, and at the time the article was supposedly written, production was going full blast, twenty-four hours a day, and practically every last family in the country was scraping up at least the hundred and fifty dollars which the cheapest model cost.

It was really an imaginative job. One of the neatest touches about it was the note of worry that ran all through the article. It was as though there were some awful problem connected with this rage for Time-Travel that the author didn't quite want to put into words. He kept hinting about it, wondering if new legislation weren't needed, and so on, but I couldn't quite figure out what he was supposed to be bothered about. Time-Travel sounded like a lot of fun to me.

"That's a wonderful job," I told Ted when I finished. "But what's the point? All that trouble—for what?"

Ted shrugged. "I don't know," he said. "No point, I guess. Did you like it?"

"I sure did."

"You can have that copy if you want. I've got another."

"Thanks," I said, and laid it in my lap. "But what did you plan to have happen next?"

"Oh," he said, "you don't want to hear any more." He seemed a little embarrassed, as though he wished he hadn't started this, and he glanced over at his wife, but she wouldn't look at him. "Matter of fact," he went on, "the story sort of peters out. I'm really not very good at that kind of thing."

"Yes," said Ann, "that's enough."

"Come on," I said to Ted. "Give."

Ted looked at me for a moment, very serious, then he shook his head again. "No," he said, "it's too hard to explain. You'd have to know a good deal about a world of the future, a world in which people are sick with the fear of self-destruction. Unimaginable weapons that could literally tear the entire solar system to pieces. Everyone living in absolute dread of the future."

"What's so hard to imagine about that?"

"Oh, hell"—he laughed. "These are peaceful times."

"They are?"

"Sure. No weapon worth mentioning except the atom and hydrogen bombs, and those in their earliest, uncomplex stages."

I laughed kind of sourly.

"All in all," he said, "these are pretty nice times to be alive in."

"Well, I'm glad you're so sure," I said.

"I am," Ted answered, and he smiled. Then he stopped smiling. "But it'll be different in another century or so, believe me. At least," he added, "that's how this friend and I figured it out in our story." He shook his head a little and went on, sort of talking to himself.

"Life will barely be worth living. Everyone working twelve, fourteen hours a day, with the major part of a man's income going for taxes, and the rest going for consumers' goods priced sky-high because of war production. Artificial scarcities, restrictions of all kinds. And hanging over everything, killing what little joy in life is left, is the virtual certainty of death and destruction. Everyone working and sacrificing for his own destruction." Ted looked up at me. "A lousy world, the world of the future, and not the way human beings were meant to live."

"Go ahead," I said, "you're doing fine."

He grinned, looked at me for a moment, then shrugged. "Okay," he said, and settled back on the porch rail. "Time-Travel hits the world the way television has hit the country today, only it happens a hundred times faster, because it's just about the only way to have any real fun. But it's a wonderful way, all right. Within less than a week after the first sets reach the market, people everywhere are going swimming after work on an untouched beach in California, say in the year 1000. Or fishing or picnicking in the Maine woods before even the Norsemen had arrived. Or standing on a hill overlooking a battlefield, watching the Crusaders have it out with the infidels."

Ted smiled. "But sometimes it's not too safe. In Newton, Kansas, a man arrives home in his living room, bleeding to death from arrow wounds. In Tallahassee a whole family disappears, their TT set turned on and humming, and they are never heard from again, and the same thing happens here and there all over the country and the world. In Chicago a man returns from a day in seventh-century France and dies in two days of the plague; everyone is worried stiff, but the disease doesn't spread. In Mill Valley, California, a man reappears in his home, his face gashed, his hand mangled, his clothes torn to shreds, and he commits suicide the following day. His wife has been stoned to death as a witch because they were fools enough to appear in a crowded eleventh-century Danish public square in modern dress, talking twenty-first-century English."

Ted grinned and winked at his wife; he was enjoying himself. I was fascinated and I think Nell was, too, whether she'd admit it or not. "But then," he went on, "warnings are soon published and televipped by all the TT manufacturers and by the government, too, and people quickly learn caution. Brief courses of instruction are published on how to conduct oneself in various times, how to simulate the dress and customs of earlier periods, what dangerous times and places to avoid, and TT really comes into its own. There are still risks, still accidents and tragedies, of course.

"Inevitably some people talk too much—the temptation is terribly strong—and they land in insane asylums or jails. Others can't stay away from the danger times and are lynched by superstitious mobs. A good many people die of the common cold, which science had eradicated and to which the human race had lost its old resistance. But there's risk in anything, and the important thing is that once again it's possible to take a *vacation*. To really get away from it all for a week, a day, or even an hour before dinner. To go back to simpler, more peaceful times when life is worth living again. And nearly every last soul in the world soon finds a way somehow to own a TT set or get access to one."

Ted looked at me, then at Nell. "Naturally, then, the inevitable happened; the only possible ending to my story. Maybe you've figured out what had to happen?"

I shook my head, and Ted looked at Nell to see if she knew; then he said, "It's easy. People simply stopped coming back. All over the world, within less than a month after TT is introduced, the same almost simultaneous thought seems to strike everyone: Why return? By this time everyone has discovered a favorite time and place in the history and geography of the world. And everybody is enthusiastic for his own particular discovery; some one century or decade, some country, city, town, island, woods or seashore, some one spot on the world's surface at a certain time that best suits his temperament. And so the same inspiration hits nearly everyone: Why not *stay* there? Why come back? To what?"

Ted slapped at a stray mosquito and said, "Within forty days' time the population of the entire world is down to less than seven million people, and nearly all of them are getting ready to leave. Suddenly the world is left to the tiny fraction of one per cent of human beings who want wars and who cause them. But the people who fight them walk out. Before the governments of the world realize what's happening—before there's time to do anything about it—the world's population is nearly gone.

"The last emergency Cabinet meeting of the U.S. government breaks up when the assembled members discover that all but one of them are themselves planning to leave for other times. In six more days the twenty-first century is deserted like a sinking ship, its population scattered thinly back through the preceding twenty-five hundred years. And of the very few who are finally left—the tiny minority who preferred the present—most are soon forced, out of sheer loneliness and the breakdown of a world, to join friends and families in earlier times."

Ted looked at us for a moment, then said, "And that, my friends, is how the world ends. On the edge of a precipice, with one foot over the edge, it stops, turns and goes back, leaving an empty earth of birds and insects, wind, rain and rusting weapons."

For maybe half a minute Ted sat staring at nothing, and no one said anything; a cricket began to chirp feebly off in the grass somewhere. Then Ted smiled. "Well," he said, "how do you like it, Al? Good story?"

"Yeah," I said slowly, still thinking about it. "Yeah," I said, "I like it fine. Why don't you write it; maybe get it published somewhere?"

"Well, I thought about that, as a matter of fact, but on the whole I prefer inventing. It's easier."

"Well, it's a good story," I said, "though there are some flaws in it of course."

"I'm sure of it," Ted said, "but what are they?"

"Well, for one thing, wouldn't people in those earlier times notice the sudden increase in population?"

"I don't think so. Spread the world's population through the thousands of preceding years, and at any one time or place it wouldn't be more than a drop in the bucket."

"Okay," I said, "but speaking of inventions, wouldn't everyone traveling back to simpler times start introducing twenty-first century inventions?"

"Not to amount to anything. You mean like space ships in seventeen seventy-six?"

"Something like that."

Ted shook his head. "It couldn't happen. Suppose *you* went back a hundred years; could you make a television set?"

"No."

"Or even a radio?"

"I might. A simple one, anyway. Maybe a crystal set."

"All right," Ted said, "suppose you did. I doubt if you could find all the materials—copper wire, for example—but suppose you managed; what would you listen to? You'd tell people it was a radio and what it was for, and they'd lock you up. You see? And what do most people know anyway about the marvelous things they use every day? Practically nothing. And even the few who do know could never find what they'd need to duplicate them, except in the actual time they belong in. The best you could do would be to introduce one or two of the very simplest things people used in your time, like a modern safety pin in Elizabethan England, if you could find the steel. And a few things like that wouldn't upset the history of the world.

"No, Al, you'd just have to take your place as best you could in the world as you found it, no matter what you knew about the future."

Well, I let it go at that. I didn't mean to get started knocking holes in Ted's story, and I went into the house and broke out beer for all hands. I liked Ted's story, though, and so did Nell, and we both said so, and after a while even Ann broke down and said she liked it, too. Then the conversation got off onto other things.

But there you are. It's like I said; the Hellenbeks were strange in some ways, but very interesting neighbors, and I was sorry to see them move away. They moved not too long afterward. They liked California fine, they said, and liked the people they'd met. But they were lonesome for old friends, people they'd grown up with, and that's understandable, of course.

So they moved to Orange, New Jersey. Some old friends were arriving there soon, they said, and the Hellenbeks were anxious to be with them. They expected them, Ted told me, sometime in the spring of 1958, and they wanted to be on hand to meet them.

There's a new couple next door now—perfectly nice people who play a good game of bridge, and we like them okay. But I don't know; after the Hellenbeks, they seem kind of dull.

The Coin Collector

". . . will let me know the number of the pattern," my wife was saying, following me down the hall toward our bedroom, "and I can knit it myself if I get the blocking done."

I think she said blocking anyway, whatever that means. And I nodded, unbuttoning my shirt as I walked. It had been hot out today and I was eager to get out of my office clothes. I began thinking about a dark-green eight-thousand-dollar sports car I'd seen during noon hour in that big show-room on Park Avenue.

". . . kind of a ribbed pattern with a matching freggel-beggis," my wife seemed to be saying as I stopped at my dresser. I tossed my shirt on the bed and turned to the mirror, arching my chest.

". . . middy collar, batten-barton sleeves with sixteen rows of smeddlycup balderdashes. . . ." Pretty good chest and shoulders I thought, staring in the mirror; I'm twenty-six years old, kind of thin-faced, not bad-looking, not good-looking.

". . . dropped hem, doppelganger waist, maroon-green, and a sort of frimble-framble daisystitch. . . ." Probably want two or three thousand bucks down on a car like that, I thought;

the payments'd be more than the rent on this whole apartment. I began emptying the change out of my pants pockets glancing at each of the coins. When I was a kid there used to be an ad in a boys' magazine: "Coin collecting can be PROFITABLE and FUN too! Why don't you start TODAY?" It explained that a 1913 Liberty-head nickel—"and many others!"—was worth thousands and I guess I'm still looking for one.

"So what do you think?" Marion was saying. "You think they'd go well together?"

"Sure, they'd look fine." I nodded at her reflection in my dresser mirror. She stood leaning in the bedroom doorway, arms folded, staring at the back of my head. I brought a dime up to my eyes for a closer look; it was minted in 1958 and had a profile of Woodrow Wilson, and I turned to Marion. "Hey, look," I said, "here's a new kind of dime—Woodrow Wilson." But she wouldn't look at my hand. She just stood there with her arms folded, glaring at me, and I said, "Now what? What have I done wrong now?" Marion wouldn't answer, and I walked to my closet and began looking for some wash pants. After a moment I said coaxingly, "Come on, Sweetfeet, what'd I do wrong?"

"Oh, Al!" she wailed. "You don't listen to me; you really don't! Half the time you don't hear a word I say!"

"Why, sure I do, honey." I was rattling the hangers, hunting for my pants. "You were talking about knitting."

"An orange sweater, I said, Al—orange. I *knew* you weren't listening and asked you how an orange sweater would go with—close your eyes."

"What?"

"No, don't turn around! And close your eyes." I closed them, and Marion said, "Now, without any peeking, because I'll see you, tell me what I'm wearing right now."

It was ridiculous. In the last five minutes, since I'd come home from the office, I must have glanced at Marion maybe two or three times. I'd kissed her when I walked into the apartment, or I was pretty sure I had. Yet standing at my closet now, eyes closed, I couldn't for the life of me say what she was wearing. I worked at it; I could actually hear the sound of her breathing just behind me and could picture her standing there, a small girl five feet three inches tall, weighing just over a hundred pounds, twenty-four years old, nice complexion, pretty face, honey-blond hair, and wearing . . . wearing . . .

"Well, am I wearing a dress, slacks, medieval armor, or standing here stark naked?"

"A dress."

"What color?"

"Ah—dark green?"

"Am I wearing stockings?"

"Yes."

"Is my hair done up, shaved off or in a pony tail?"

"Done up."

"O.K., you can look now."

Of course the instant I turned around to look, I remembered. There she stood, eyes blazing, her bare foot angrily tapping the floor, and she was wearing sky-blue wash slacks and a white cotton blouse. As she swung away to walk out of the room and down the hall, her pony tail was bobbing furiously.

Well, brother—and you, too, sister—unless the rice is still in your hair you know what came next—the hurt indignant silence. I got into slacks, short-sleeved shirt and huaraches, strolled into the living room, and there on the davenport sat Madame Defarge grimly studying the list, disguised as a magazine, of next day's guillotine victims. I knew whose name headed the list, and I walked straight to the kitchen, mixed up some booze in tall glasses, and found a screw driver in a kitchen drawer.

In the living room, coldly ignored by what had once been my radiant laughing bride, I set the drinks on the coffee table, reached behind Marion's magazine, and gripped her chin between thumb and forefinger. The magazine dropped and I instantly inserted the tip of the screw driver between her front teeth, pried open her mouth, picked up a glass and tried to pour in some booze. She started to laugh, spilling some down her front, and I grinned, handing her the glass, and picked up mine. Sitting down beside her, I saluted Marion with my glass, then took a delightful sip and as it hurried to my sluggish blood stream I could feel the happy corpuscles dive in, laughing and shouting, and felt able to cope with the next item on the agenda which followed immediately.

"You don't love me any more," said Marion.

"Oh, yes, I do." I leaned over to kiss her neck, glancing around the room over her shoulder.

"Oh, no, you don't. Not really."

"Oh, yes, I do. Really. Honey, where's the book I was reading last night?"

"There! You see! All you want to do is read all the time! You never want to go out! The honeymoon's certainly over around here, all right!"

"No, it isn't, Sweetknees, not at all. I feel exactly the way I did the day I proposed to you; I honestly do. Was there any mail?"

"Just some ads and a bill. You used to listen to every word I said before we were married and you always noticed what I wore and you complimentd me and you sent me flowers and you brought me little surprises and"—suddenly she sat bolt upright—"remember those cute little notes you used to send me! I'd find them all the time," she said sadly, staring past my shoulder, her eyes widening wistfully. "Tucked in my purse maybe"—she smiled mournfully—"or in a glove. Or they'd come to the office on post cards, even in telegrams a couple times. All the other girls used to say they were just darling." She swung to face me. "Honey, why don't you ever . . ."

"Help!" I said. "Help, help!"

"What do you mean?" Marion demanded coolly, and I tried to explain.

"Look, honey," I said brisky, putting an arm companionably around her shoulders, "we've been married four years. Of course the honeymoon's over! What kind of imbeciles," I asked with complete reasonableness, "would we be if it weren't? I love you, sure," I assured her, shrugging a shoulder. "Of course. You bet. Always glad to see you; any wife of old Al Pullen is a wife of mine! But after four years I walk up the stairs when I come home; I no longer run up three at a time. That's life," I said, clapping her cheerfully on the back. "Even four-alarm fires eventually die down, you know." I smiled at her fondly. "And as for cute little notes tucked in your purse—help, help!" I should have known better, I guess; there are certain things you just can't seem to explain to a woman.

I had trouble getting to sleep that night—the davenport is much too short for me—and it was around two forty-five before I finally sank into a kind of exhausted broken-backed coma. Breakfast next morning, you can believe me, was a glum affair at the town home of Mr. and Mrs. Alfred E. Pullen, well-known, devoted couple.

Who can say whether the events of the night before affected those which now followed? I certainly couldn't; I was too tired, dragging home from the office along Third Avenue, heading uptown from Thirty-fourth Street about five thirty the next evening. I was tired, depressed, irritated, and in no hurry at all to get home. It was hot and muggy outside and I was certain Marion would give me cold cuts for supper—and all evening long, for that matter. My tie was pulled down, my collar open, hat shoved back, coat slung over one shoulder, and trudging along the sidewalk there I got to wishing things were different.

I didn't care how, exactly—just different. For example, how would things be right now, it occurred to me, if I'd majored in creative botany at college instead of physical ed? Or what would I be doing at this very moment if I'd gone to Siam with Tom Biehler that time? Or if I'd got the job with Enterprises, Incorporated, instead of Serv-Eez? Or if I hadn't broken off with what's-her-name, that big, black-haired girl who could sing "Japanese Sandman" through her nose?

At Thirty-sixth Street I stopped at the corner newsstand, plunking my dime down on the counter before the man who ran it; we knew each other long since, though I don't think we've ever actually spoken. Glancing at me, he scooped up my dime, grabbed a paper from one of the stacks and folded it as he handed it to me; and I nodded my thanks, tucking it under my arm, and walked on. And that's when it happened; I glanced up at a brick building kitty-corner across the street and there on a blank side wall three or four stories up was a painted advertisement—a narrow-waisted bottle filled with a reddish-brown beverage and lying half buried in a bed of blue-white ice. Painted just over the bottle in a familiar script were the words, "DRINK COCO-COOLA."

Do you see? It didn't say "Coca-Cola." Not quite. And staring up at that painted sign, I knew it was no sign painter's mistake. They don't make mistakes like that; not on great big outdoor signs that take a couple of men several days to paint. I knew it couldn't possibly be a rival soft drink either; the spelling and entire appearance of this ad were too close to those of Coca-Cola. No, I knew that sign was meant to read "Coco-Coola," and turning to walk on finally—well, it may strike you as insane what I felt certain I knew from just the sight of that painted sign high above a New York street.

But within two steps that feeling was confirmed. I glanced out at the street beside me; it was rush hour and the cars streamed past, clean cars and dirty ones, old and new. But every one of them was painted a single color only, mostly black, and there wasn't a tail fin or strip of chromium in sight. These were modern, fast, good-looking cars, you understand, but utterly different in design from any I'd ever before seen. The traffic lights on Third Avenue clicked to red, the cars slowed and stopped, and now as I walked along past them I was able to read some of their names. There were a Ford, a Buick, two Wintons, a Stutz, a Cadillac, a Dort, a Kissel, an Oldsmobile, and at least four or five small Pierce-Arrows. Then, glancing down Thirty-seventh Street as I passed it, I saw a billboard advertising Picayune Cigarettes: AMERICA'S LARGEST-SELLING BRAND. And now a Third Avenue bus dragged past me, crammed with people as usual this time of day, but it was shaped a little differently and it was painted blue and white.

I spun suddenly around on the walk, looking frantically for the Empire State Building. But it was there, all right, just where it was supposed to be, and I actually sighed with relief. It was shorter, though, by a good ten stories at least. When had all this happened? I wondered dazedly and opened my paper, but there was nothing unusual in it—till I noticed the name at the top of the page. New York *Sun,* it said, and I stood on the sidewalk gaping at it because the *Sun* hasn't been published in New York for years.

Do you understand now? I did, finally, but of course I like

to read—when I get the chance, that is—and I'm extremely well grounded in science from all the science fiction I've read. So I was certain, presently, that I knew what had happened; maybe you've figured it out too.

Years ago someone had to decide on a name for a new soft drink and finally picked "Coca-Cola." But certainly he considered other possible alternatives; and if the truth could be known, I'll bet one of them was "Coco-Coola." It's not a bad name—sounds cool and refreshing—and he may have come very close to deciding on it.

And how come Ford, Buick, Chevrolet, and Oldsmobile survived while the Moon, Willys-Knight, Hupmobile, and Kissel didn't? Well, at some point or other maybe a decision was made by the men who ran the Kissel Company, for example, which might just as easily have been made another way. If it had, maybe Kissel would have survived and be a familiar sight today.

Instead of Lucky Strikes, Camels, and Chesterfields, we might be buying chiefly Picayunes, Sweet Caporals, and Piedmonts. We might not have the Japanese beetle or the atom bomb. While the biggest newspaper in New York could be the *Sun,* and George Coopernagel might be President. If—what would the world be like right now, what would you or I be doing?—if only things in the past had happened just a tiny bit differently. There are thousands of possibilities, of course; there are millions and trillions. There is every conceivable kind of world, in fact; and a theory of considerable scientific standing—Einstein believed it—is that these other possible worlds actually exist—all of them, side by side and simultaneously with the one we happen to be familiar with.

I believed it too now, naturally; I knew what had happened, all right. Walking along Third Avenue through the late afternoon on my way home from the office, I had come to one of the tiny points where two of these alternate worlds intersected somehow. And I had walked off out of one into another slightly altered, somewhat different world of "If" that was every bit as real and which existed quite as much as the one I'd just left.

For maybe a block I walked on, stunned but with a growing curiosity and excitement—because it had occurred to me to wonder where I was going. I was walking on with a definite purpose and destination, I realized; and when a traffic light beside me clicked to green, I took the opportunity to cross La Guardia Avenue, as it was labeled now, and then continue west along Thirty-ninth Street. I was going somewhere, no doubt about that; and in the instant of wondering where I felt a chill along my spine. Because suddenly I knew.

All the memories of my life in another world, you understand, still existed in my mind, from distant past to the present. But beginning with the moment that I had turned from the newsstand to glance up at that painted sign, another set of memories—an alternate set of memories of my other life in this alternate world—began stirring to life underneath the first. But they were dim and faint yet, out of focus. I knew where I was going—vaguely—and I no more had to think how to get there than any other man on his way home from work. My legs simply moved in an old familiar pattern, carrying me up to the double glass doors of a big apartment building, and the doorman said, "Evening, Mr. Pullen. Hot today."

"You said it, Charley," I answered and walked on into the lobby. Then my legs were carrying me up the stairs to the second floor, then down a corridor to an apartment door which stood open. And just as I did every night, I realized, I walked into the living room, tossing my copy of the *Sun* to the davenport. I was wearing a suit I'd never seen before, I noticed, but it fitted me perfectly, of course, and was a little worn.

"Hi, I'm home," I heard my voice call out as always. And at one and the same time I knew, with complete and time-dulled familiarity—and also wondered with intense and fascinating curiosity—who in the world was going to answer; who in *this* world?

An oven door slammed in the kitchen as I turned to hang up my suit coat in the hall closet as always, then footsteps sounded on the wood floor between the kitchen and the living room. And as she said, "Hi, darling," I turned to see my wife walking toward me.

I had to admire my taste in this world. She was a big girl, tall and not quite slim; black-haired and with a very fair complexion; quite a pretty face with a single vertical frown line between her brows; and she had an absolutely gorgeous figure with long handsome legs. "Why, hel-lo," I said slowly. "What a preposterously good-looking female you are!"

Her jaw dropped in simple astonishment, her blue eyes narrowing suspiciously. I held my arms wide then, walking toward her delightedly, and, while she accepted my embrace, she drew back to sniff my breath. She couldn't draw back very far, though, because my embrace—I simply couldn't help this—was tight and close; this fine-looking girl was a spectacular armful. "Now I know why I go to the office every day," I was saying as I nuzzled her lovely white neck, an extremely agreeable sensation. "There had to be a reason and now I know what it is. It's so I can come home to this."

"Al, what in the world is the matter with you?" she said. Her voice was still astonished but she'd quit trying to draw back.

"Nothing you can't remedy," I said, "in a variety of delightful ways," and I kissed her again.

"Honey," she murmured after a considerable time, "I have to fix supper," and she made a little token effort to get away.

"Supper can wait," I answered, and my voice was a full octave deeper, "but I can't." Again I kissed her, hard and eagerly, full on the lips. Her great big beautiful blue eyes widened in amazement—then they slowly closed and she smiled languorously.

Marion's face abruptly rose up in my mind. There in the forefront of my consciousness and conscience suddenly was her betrayed and indignant face, every bit as vivid as though she'd actually walked in through the door to discover this sultry brunette in my arms; and I could feel my face flame with guilt. Because I couldn't kid myself, I couldn't possibly deny the intensity of the pleasure I'd felt at this girl in my arms. I knew how very close I'd come to betraying Marion and I felt terribly ashamed and stood wondering—this long length of glorious girlhood still in my arms—how to end the situation with charm and grace. A moment later her eyes opened and she looked up at me questioningly, those full ripe moist lips slightly apart. "Hate to say this," I said then, sniffing the air thoughtfully, "but seems to me I smell something burning—besides me."

"Oh!"—she let out a little shriek and as she ran to the kitchen I actually closed my eyes and sighed with a terrible relief. I didn't know how I'd walked into this other alternate world or how I could leave it, but Marion was alive in my mind while the world around me seemed unreal. In the kitchen I heard the oven door open, heard water run in the sink, then the momentary sizzle of cooking meat; and I walked quickly to the davenport and snatched up my copy of the *Sun*.

As I raised it to my face the tap of high heels sounded on the wood floor just outside the kitchen door. There was silence as they crossed the rug toward me, then the davenport cushion beside me sank; I felt a deliciously warm breath on my cheek, and I had to lower my trembling rattling newspaper and smile into the sloe eyes of the creature beside me.

Once again—my head slowly shaking in involuntary approval—I had to admire my own good taste; this was not a homely woman. "I turned the oven down," she murmured. "It might be better to have dinner a little later. When it gets cooler," she added softly.

I nodded quickly. "Good idea. Paper says it's the hottest day in five hundred years," I babbled. "Doctors advise complete immobility."

But the long-legged beauty beside me wasn't listening. "So I'm the reason you like to come home, am I?" she breathed into my ear. "It's been a long time, darling, since you said anything like that."

"H'm'm," I murmured and nodded frantically at the paper in my hands. "I see they're going to tear down City Hall," but she was blowing gently in my ear now. Then she pulled the *Sun* from my paralyzed fingers, tossed it over her shoulder, and leaned toward me. *Marion!* I was shrieking silently. *Help!* Then the raven-haired girl beside me had her arms around my neck and I simply did not know what to do; I thought of pretending to faint, claiming sunstroke.

Then with the blinding force of a revelation it came to me. Through no fault of my own I was in another world, another life. The girl in my arms—somehow that's where she was now—was singing softly, almost inaudibly. It took me a moment to recognize the tune. Then finally I knew, finally I recognized this magnificent girl. " 'Just a Japanese Sandman,' " she was singing softly through her lovely nose and now I remembered fully everything about the alternate world I was in. I hadn't broken off with this girl at all—not in this particular world! Matter of fact, I suddenly realized, I'd never even met Marion in this world. It was even possible, it occurred to me now, that she'd never been born. In any case, this was the girl I'd married in this world. No denying it, this was my wife here beside me with her arms around my neck; we'd been married three years, in fact. And now I knew what to do—perfectly well.

Oh, boy! What a wonderful time Vera and I had in the months that followed. My work at the office was easy, no strain at all. I seemed to have an aptitude for it and, just as I'd always suspected, I made rather more money at Enterprises, Incorporated, than that Serv-Eez outfit ever paid in its life. More than once, too, I left the office early, since no one seemed to mind, just to hurry back home—leaping up the stairs three at a time—to that lovely big old Vera again. And at least once every week I'd bring home a load of books under my arm, because she loved to read, just like me; and I'd made a wonderful discovery about this alternate world.

Life, you understand, was different in its details. The San Francisco Giants had won the 1962 Series, for example; the Second Avenue El was still up; Yucatan gum was the big favorite; television was good; and several extremely prominent people whose names would astound you were in jail. But basically the two worlds were much the same. Drugstores, for example, looked and smelled just about the same; and one night on the way home from work I stopped in at a big drugstore to look over the racks of paperback books and made a marvelous discovery.

There on the revolving metal racks were the familiar rows of glossy little books, every one of which, judging from the covers, seemed to be about an abnormally well-developed girl. Turning the rack slowly I saw books by William Faulkner, Collin Wilcox, and one G. Montizambert, which I'd read and liked. Then, down near the bottom of the rack my eye was caught by the words, "By Mark Twain." The cover showed an old side-wheeler steamboat, and the title was *South from Cairo.* A reprint fitted out with a new title, I thought, feeling annoyed; and I picked up the book to see just which of Mark Twain's it really was. I've read every book he wrote—*Huckleberry Finn* at least a dozen times since I discovered it when I was eleven years old.

But the text of this book was new to me. It seemed to be an account, told in the first person by a young man of twenty, of his application for a job on a Mississippi steamboat. And then, from the bottom of a page, a name leaped out at me. " 'Finn, sir,' I answered the captain," the text read, " 'but mostly they call me Huckleberry.' "

For a moment I just stood there in the drugstore with my mouth hanging open; then I turned the little book in my hands. On the back cover was a photograph of Mark Twain—the familiar shock of white hair, the mustache, that wise old face. But underneath this the brief familiar account of his life ended with saying that he had died in 1918 in Mill Valley, California. Mark Twain had lived eight years longer in this alternate world, and had written—well, I didn't yet know how many more books he had written in this wonderful world but I knew I was going to find out. And my hand was trembling as I walked up to the cashier and gave her two bits for my priceless copy of *South from Cairo.*

I love reading in bed, and that night I read a good half of my new Mark Twain in bed with Vera, and afterward—well, afterward she fixed me a nice cool Tom Collins. And oh, boy, this was the life all right.

In the weeks that followed—that lanky length of violet-eyed womanhood cuddled up beside me, singing softly through her nose—I read a new novel by Ernest Hemingway, the best of all, I think. I read a serious wonderfully good novel by James Thurber, and something else I'd been hoping to find for years—the sequel to a marvelous book called *Delilah,* by Marcus Goodrich. In fact, I read some of the best reading since Gutenberg kicked things off—a good deal of it aloud to Vera, who enjoyed it as much as I did. I read *Mistress Murder,* a hilarious detective story by George S. Kaufman; *The Queen Is Dead,* by George Bernard Shaw; *Time and Again,* an odd kind of book by someone or other I never heard of, but not too bad; a wonderful novel by Allen Marple; a group of fine stories about the advertising business by Alfred Eichler; a terrific play by Orson Welles; and a whole new volume of Sherlock Holmes stories by A. Conan Doyle.

For four or five months, as Vera rather aptly remarked, I thought, it was like a second honeymoon. I did all the wonderful little things, she said, that I used to do on our honeymoon and before we were married; I even thought up some new ones. And then—all of a sudden one night—I wanted to go to a night club.

All of a sudden I wanted to get out of the house in the evening and do something else for a change. Vera was astonished—wanted to know what was the matter with me, which is typical of a woman. If you don't react precisely the same way day after endless day, they think something must be wrong with you. They'll even insist on it. I didn't want any black-cherry ice cream for dessert, I told Vera one night at dinner. Why not, she wanted to know—which is idiotic if you stop to think about it. I didn't want any because I didn't want any, that's all! But being a woman she had to have a reason; so I said, "Because I don't like it."

"But of course you like it," she said. "You always used to like it!"

You see what I mean? Anyway, we did go to this night

club, but it wasn't much fun. Vera got sleepy, and we left, and were home before twelve. Then she wasn't sleepy but I was. Couple nights later I came home from the office and was changing my clothes; she said something or other and I didn't hear her and didn't answer, and we actually had a little argument. She wanted to know why I always looked at every coin in my pocket like an idiot every time I changed clothes. I explained quietly enough; told her about the ad I used to read as a kid and how I was still looking for a 1913 Liberty-head nickel worth thousands of dollars, which was the truth.

But it wasn't the whole truth. As I looked through the coins I'd collected in my pocket during the day—the Woodrow Wilson dimes, the Grover Cleveland pennies, the nickels with George Coopernagel's profile, and all the other familiar coins of the world I now lived in—I understood something that had puzzled me once.

These other alternate worlds in which we also live intersect here and there—at a corner newsstand, for example, on Third Avenue in New York and at many another place, too, no doubt. And from these intersecting places every once in a while something from one of these worlds—a Woodrow Wilson dime, for example—will stray into another one. I'd found such a dime and when I happened to plank it down on the counter of that little newsstand there at an intersection of the two alternate worlds, that dime bought a newspaper in the world it belonged in. And I walked off into that world with the New York *Sun* under my arm. I knew this now, and I'd known it long since. I understood it finally, but I didn't tell Vera. I simply told her I was looking for a 1913 Liberty-head nickel. I didn't tell her I was also looking for a Roosevelt dime.

I found one, too. One night finally, sure enough, there it lay in my palm—a dime with the profile of Franklin D. Roosevelt on its face. And when I slapped it down on the counter of the little newsstand next evening, there at the intersection of two alternate worlds, I was trembling. The man snatched up a paper, folding it as he handed it to me, and I tucked it under my arm and walked on for three or four steps, hardly daring to breathe. Then I opened the paper and looked at it. New York *World-Telegram,* the masthead read, and I began to run—all the way to Forty-fourth Street, then east to First Avenue, and then up three flights of stairs.

I could hardly talk I was so out of breath when I burst into the apartment, but I managed to gasp out the only word that mattered. "Marion!" I said and grabbed her to me, almost choking her, because my arms hit the back of her head about where Vera's shoulders would have been. But she managed to talk, struggling to break loose, her voice sort of muffled against my coat.

"Al!" she said. "What in the world is the matter with you?"

For her, of course, I'd been here last night and every night for the months and years past. And of course, back in this world, I remembered it, too, but dimly, mistily. I stepped back now and looked down at the marvelous tiny size of Marion, at that wonderful, petite figure, at her exquisite and fragile blond beauty. "Nothing's the matter with me," I said, grinning down at her. "It's just that I've got a beautiful wife and was in a hurry to get home to her. Anything wrong with that?"

There wasn't; not a thing, and—well, it's been wonderful, my life with Marion, ever since. It's an exciting life; we're out three and four nights a week, I guess—dancing, the theater, visiting friends, going to night clubs, having dinner out, even bowling. It's the way things used to be, as Marion has aptly said. In fact, she remarked recently, it's like a second honeymoon, and she's wonderfully happy these days and so am I.

Oh, sometimes I'm a little tired at night lately. There are times after a tough day at Serv-Eez when I'd almost rather stay home and read a good book; it's been quite a while since I did. But I don't worry about that. Because the other night, about two thirty in the morning, just back from the Mirimba, standing at my dresser looking through the coins in my pocket, I found it—another Woodrow Wilson dime. You come across them every once in a while, I've noticed, if you just keep your eyes open; Wilson dimes, Ulysses Grant quarters, Coopernagel nickels. And I've got my Wilson dime safely tucked away, and—well, I'm sure Vera, that lithe-limbed creature, will be mighty glad to see her husband suddenly acting his old self once again. I imagine it'll be like a third honeymoon. Just as—in time—it will be for Marion.

So there you are, brother, coin collecting can be profitable. And FUN too! Why don't you start—tonight!

Of Missing Persons

Walk in as though it were an ordinary travel bureau, the stranger I'd met at a bar had told me. *Ask a few ordinary questions—about a trip you're planning, a vacation, anything like that. Then hint about The Folder a little, but whatever you do, don't mention it directly; wait till he brings it up himself. And if he doesn't, you might as well forget it. If you can. Because you'll never see it; you're not the type, that's all. And if you ask about it, he'll just look at you as though he doesn't know what you're talking about.*

I rehearsed it all in my mind, over and over, but what seems possible at night over a beer isn't easy to believe on a raw, rainy day, and I felt like a fool, searching the store fronts for the street number I'd memorized. It was noon hour, West 42nd Street, New York, rainy and windy; and like half the men around me, I walked with a hand on my hatbrim, wearing an old trench coat, head bent into the slanting rain, and the world was real and drab, and this was hopeless.

Anyway, I couldn't help thinking, who am I to see The Folder, even if there is one? Name? I said to myself, as though I were already being asked. It's Charley Ewell, and

I'm a young guy who works in a bank; a teller. I don't like the job; I don't make much money, and I never will. I've lived in New York for over three years and haven't many friends. What the hell, there's really nothing to say—I see more movies than I want to, read too many books, and I'm sick of meals alone in restaurants. I have ordinary abilities, looks and thoughts. Does that suit you; do I qualify?

Now I spotted it, the address in the two-hundred block, an old, pseudo-modernized office building, tired, outdated, refusing to admit it but unable to hide it. New York has a lot of them west of Fifth.

I pushed through the brass-framed glass doors into the tiny lobby, paved with freshly mopped, permanently dirty tile. The green-painted walls were lumpy from old plaster repairs; in a chrome frame hung a little wall directory—white celluloid easily-changed letters on a black felt background. There were some twenty-odd names, and I found "Acme Travel Bureau" second on the list, between "A-1 Mimeo" and "Ajax Magic Supplies." I pressed the bell beside the old-style open-grille elevator door; it rang high up in the shaft. There was a long pause, then a thump, and the heavy chains began rattling slowly down toward me, and I almost turned and left—this was insane.

But upstairs the Acme office had divorced itself from the atmosphere of the building. I pushed open the pebble-glass door, walked in, and the big square room was bright and clean, fluorescent-lighted. Beside the wide double windows, behind a counter, stood a tall gray-haired, grave-looking man a telephone at his ear. He glanced up, nodded to beckon me in, and I felt my heart pumping—he fitted the description exactly. "Yes, United Air Lines," he was saying into the phone. "Flight"—he glanced at a paper on the glass-topped counter—"seven-o-three, and I suggest you check in forty minutes early."

Standing before him now, I waited, leaning on the counter, glancing around; he was the man, all right, and yet this was just an ordinary travel agency: big bright posters on the walls, metal floor racks full of folders, printed schedules under the glass on the counter. This is just what it looks like and nothing else, I thought, and again I felt like a fool.

"Can I help you?" Behind the counter the tall gray-haired man was smiling at me, replacing the phone, and suddenly I was terribly nervous.

"Yes." I stalled for time, unbuttoning my raincoat. Then I looked up at him again and said, "I'd like to—get away." You fool, that's too fast! I told myself. Don't rush it! I watched in a kind of panic to see what effect my answer had had, but he didn't flick an eyelash.

"Well, there are a lot of places to go," he said politely. From under the counter he brought out a long, slim folder and laid it on the glass, turning it right side up for me. "Fly to Buenos Aires—Another World!" it said in a double row of pale green letters across the top.

I looked at it long enough to be polite. It showed a big silvery plane banking over a harbor at night, a moon shining on the water, mountains in the background. Then I just shook my head; I was afraid to talk, afraid I'd say the wrong thing.

"Something quieter, maybe?" He brought out another folder: thick old tree trunks, rising way up out of sight, sunbeams slanting down through them—"The Virgin Forests of Maine, via Boston and Maine Railroad." "Or"—he laid a third folder on the glass—"Bermuda is nice just now." This one said, "Bermuda, Old World in the New."

I decided to risk it. "No," I said, and shook my head. "What

I'm really looking for is a permanent place. A new place to live and settle down in." I stared directly into his eyes. "For the rest of my life." Then my nerve failed me, and I tried to think of a way to backtrack.

But he only smiled pleasantly and said, "I don't know why we can't advise you on that." He leaned forward on the counter, resting on his forearms, hands clasped; he had all the time in the world for me, his posture conveyed. "What are you looking for; what do you want?"

I held my breath, then said it. "Escape."

"From what?"

"Well——" Now I hesitated; I'd never put it into words before. "From New York, I'd say. And cities in general. From worry. And fear. And the things I read in my newspapers. From loneliness." And then I couldn't stop, though I knew I was talking too much, the words spilling out. "From never doing what I really want to do or having much fun. From selling my days just to stay alive. From life itself—the way it is today, at least." I looked straight at him and said softly, "From the world."

Now he was frankly staring, his eyes studying my face intently with no pretense of doing anything else, and I knew that in a moment he'd shake his head and say, "Mister, you better get to a doctor." But he didn't. He continued to stare, his eyes examining my forehead now. He was a big man, his gray hair crisp and curling, his lined face very intelligent, very kind; he looked the way ministers should look; he looked the way all fathers should look.

He lowered his gaze to look into my eyes and beyond them; he studied my mouth, my chin, the line of my jaw, and I had the sudden conviction that without any difficulty he was learning a great deal about me, more than I knew myself. Suddenly he smiled and placed both elbows on the counter, one hand grasping the other fist and gently massaging it. "Do you like people? Tell the truth, because I'll know if you aren't."

"Yes. It isn't easy for me to relax though, and be myself, and make friends."

He nodded gravely, accepting that. "Would you say you're a reasonably decent kind of man?"

"I guess so; I think so." I shrugged.

"Why?"

I smiled wryly; this was hard to answer. "Well—at least when I'm not, I'm usually sorry about it."

He grinned at that, and considered it for a moment or so. Then he smiled—deprecatingly, as though he were about to tell a little joke that wasn't too good. "You know," he said casually, "we occasionally get people in here who seem to be looking for pretty much what you are. So just as a sort of little joke——"

I couldn't breathe. This was what I'd been told he would say if he thought I might do.

"——we've worked up a little folder. We've even had it printed. Simply for our own amusement, you understand. And for occasional clients like you. So I'll have to ask you to look at it here if you're interested. It's not the sort of thing we'd care to have generally known."

I could barely whisper, "I'm interested."

He fumbled under the counter, then brought out a long thin folder, the same size and shape as the others, and slid it over the glass toward me.

I looked at it, pulling it closer with a finger tip, almost afraid to touch it. The cover was dark blue, the shade of a night sky, and across the top in white letters it said, "Visit Enchanting Verna!" The blue cover was sprinkled with white dots—stars—and in the lower left corner was a globe, the world, half surrounded by clouds. At the upper right, just under the word "Verna," was a star larger and brighter than the others; rays shot out from it, like those from a star on a Christmas card. Across the bottom of the cover it said, "Romantic Verna, where life is the way it *should* be." There was a little arrow beside the legend, meaning Turn the page.

I turned, and the folder was like most travel folders inside—there were pictures and text, only these were about "Verna" instead of Paris, or Rome, or the Bahamas. And it was beautifully printed; the pictures looked real. What I mean is, you've seen color stereopticon pictures? Well, that's what these were like, only better, far better. In one picture you could see dew glistening on grass, and it looked wet. In another, a tree trunk seemed to curve out of the page, in perfect detail, and it was a shock to touch it and feel smooth paper instead of the rough actuality of bark. Miniature human faces, in a third picture, seemed about to speak, the lips moist and alive, the eyeballs shining, the actual texture of skin right there on paper; and it seemed impossible, as you stared, that the people wouldn't move and speak.

I studied a large picture spreading across the upper half of two open pages. It seemed to have been taken from the top of a hill; you saw the land dropping away at your feet far down into a valley, then rising up again, way over on the other side. The slopes of both hills were covered with forest, and the color was beautiful, perfect; there were miles of green, majestic trees, and you knew as you looked that this forest was virgin, almost untouched. Curving through the floor of the valley, far below, ran a stream, blue from the sky in most places; here and there, where the current broke around massive boulders, the water was foaming white; and again it seemed that if you'd only look closely enough you'd be certain to see that stream move and shine in the sun. In clearings beside the stream there were shake-roofed cabins, some of logs, some of brick or adobe. The caption under the picture simply said, "The Colony."

"Fun fooling around with a thing like that," the man behind the counter murmured, nodding at the folder in my hands. "Relieves the monotony. Attractive-looking place, isn't it?"

I could only nod dumbly, lowering my eyes to the picture again because that picture told you even more than just what you saw. I don't know how you knew this, but you realized, staring at that forest-covered valley, that this was very much the way America once looked when it was new. And you knew this was only a part of a whole land of unspoiled, unharmed forests, where every stream ran pure; you were seeing what people, the last of them dead over a century ago, had once looked at in Kentucky and Wisconsin and the old Northwest. And you knew that if you could breathe in that air you'd feel it flow into your lungs sweeter than it's been anywhere on earth for a hundred and fifty years.

Under that picture was another, of six or eight people on a beach—the shore of a lake, maybe, or the river in the picture above. Two children were squatting on their haunches, dabbling in the water's edge, and in the foreground a half circle of adults were sitting, kneeling, or squatting in comfortable balance on the yellow sand. They were talking, several were smoking, and most of them held half-filled coffee cups; the sun was bright, you knew the air was balmy and that it was morning, just after breakfast. They were smiling, one woman talking, the others listening. One man had half risen from his squatting position to skip a stone out onto the surface of the water.

You knew this: that they were spending twenty minutes or so down on that beach after breakfast before going to work, and you knew they were friends and that they did this every day. You knew—I tell you, you *knew*—that they liked their work, all of them, whatever it was; that there was no forced hurry or pressure about it. And that—well, that's all, I guess; you just knew that every day after breakfast these families spent a leisurely half hour sitting and talking, there in the morning sun, down on that wonderful beach.

I'd never seen anything like their faces before. They were ordinary enough in looks, the people in that picture—pleasant, more or less familiar types. Some were young, in their twenties; others were in their thirties; one man and woman seemed around fifty. But the faces of the youngest couple were completely unlined, and it occurred to me then that they had been born there, and that it was a place where no one worried or was ever afraid. The others, the older ones, there were lines in their foreheads, grooves around their mouths, but you felt that the lines were no longer deepening, that they were healed and untroubled scars. And in the faces of the oldest couple was a look of—I'd say it was a look of permanent *relief*. Not one of those faces bore a trace of malice; these people were *happy*. But even more than that, you knew they'd *been* happy, day after day after day for a long, long time, and that they always would be, and they knew it.

I wanted to join them. The most desperate longing roared up in me from the bottom of my soul to *be* there—on that beach, after breakfast, with those people in the sunny morning—and I could hardly stand it. I looked up at the man behind the counter and managed to smile. "This is—very interesting."

"Yes," he smiled back, then shook his head in amusement. "We've had customers so interested, so carried away, that they didn't want to talk about anything else." He laughed. "They actually wanted to know rates, details, everything."

I nodded to show I understood and agreed with them. "And I suppose you've worked out a whole story to go with this?" I glanced at the folder in my hands.

"Oh, yes. What would you like to know?"

"These people," I said softly, and touched the picture of the group on the beach. "What do they do?"

"They work; everyone does." He took a pipe from his pocket. "They simply live their lives doing what they like. Some study. We have, according to our little story," he added, and smiled, "a very fine library. Some of our people farm, some write, some make things with their hands. Most of them raise children, and—well, they work at whatever it is they really want to do."

"And if there isn't anything they really want to do?"

He shook his head. "There is always something, for everyone, that he really wants to do. It's just that here there is so rarely time to find out what it is." He brought out a tobacco pouch and, leaning on the counter, began filling his pipe, his eyes level with mine, looking at me gravely. "Life is simple there, and it's serene. In some ways, the good ways, it's like the early pioneering communities here in your country, but without the drudgery that killed people young. There is electricity. There are washing machines, vacuum cleaners, plumbing, modern bathrooms, and modern medicine, very modern. But there are no radios, television, telephones, or automobiles. Distances are small, and people live and work in small communities. They raise or make most of the things they use. Every man builds his own house, with all the help he needs from his neighbors. Their recreation is their own, and there is a great deal of it, but there is no recreation for sale, nothing you buy a ticket to. They have dances, card parties, weddings, christenings, birthday celebrations, harvest parties. There are swimming and sports of all kinds. There is conversation, a lot of it, plenty of joking and laughter. There is a great deal of visiting and sharing of meals, and each day is well filled and well spent. There are no pressures, economic or social, and life holds few threats. Every man, woman and child is a happy person." After a moment he smiled. "I'm repeating the text, of course, in our little joke." He nodded at the folder.

"Of course," I murmured, and looked down at the folder again, turning a page. "Homes in The Colony," said a caption, and there, true and real, were a dozen or so pictures of the interiors of what must have been the cabins I'd seen in the first photographs, or others like them. There were living rooms, kitchens, dens, patios. Many of the homes seemed to be furnished in a kind of Early American style, except that it looked—authentic, as though those rocking chairs, cupboards, tables and hooked rugs had been made by the people themselves, taking their time and making them well and beautifully. Others of the interiors seemed modern in style; one showed a definite Oriental influence.

All of them had, plainly and unmistakably, one quality in common: You knew as you looked at them that these rooms were *home,* really home, to the people who lived in them. On the wall of one living room, over the stone fireplace, hung a hand-stitched motto: "There Is No Place Like Home," but the words didn't seem quaint or amusing, they didn't seem old-fashioned, resurrected or copied from a past that was gone. They seemed real; they belonged; those words were nothing more or less than a simple expression of true feeling and fact.

"Who are you?" I lifted my head from the folder to stare into the man's eyes.

He lighted his pipe, taking his time, sucking the match flame down into the bowl, eyes glancing up at me. "It's in the text," he said then, "on the back page. We—that is to say, the people of Verna, the original inhabitants—are people like yourself. Verna is a planet of air, sun, land and sea, like this one. And of the same approximate temperature. So life evolved there, of course, just about as it has here, though rather earlier; and we are people like you. There are trivial anatomical differences, but nothing important. We read and enjoy your James Thurber, John Clayton, Rabelais, Allen Marple, Hemingway, Grimm, Mark Twain, Alan Nelson. We like your chocolate, which we didn't have, and a great deal of your music. And you'd like many of the things we have. Our thoughts, though, and the great aims and directions of our history and development have been—drastically different from yours." He smiled and blew out a puff of smoke. "Amusing fantasy, isn't it?"

"Yes." I knew I sounded abrupt, and I hadn't stopped to smile; the words were spilling out. "And where is Verna?"

"Light years away, by your measurements."

I was suddenly irritated, I didn't know why. "A little hard to get to, then, wouldn't it be?"

For a moment he looked at me; then he turned to the window beside him. "Come here," he said, and I walked around the counter to stand beside him. "There, off to the left"—he put a hand on my shoulder and pointed with his pipe stem—"are two apartment buildings, built back to back. The entrance to one is on Fifth Avenue, the entrance to the other on Sixth. See them? In the middle of the block; you can just see their roofs."

I nodded, and he said, "A man and his wife live on the fourteenth floor of one of those buildings. A wall of their living room is the back wall of the building. They have friends on the fourteenth floor of the other building, and a wall of *their* living room is the back wall of *their* building. These two couples live, in other words, within two feet of one another, since the back building walls actually touch."

The big man smiled. "But when the Robinsons want to visit the Bradens, they walk from their living room to the front door. Then they walk down a long hall to the elevators. They ride fourteen floors down; then, in the street, they must walk around to the next block. And the city blocks there are long; in bad weather they have sometimes actually taken a cab. They walk into the other building, they go on through the lobby, ride up fourteen floors, walk down a hall, ring a bell, and are finally admitted into their friends' living room—only two feet from their own."

The big man turned back to the counter, and I walked around it to the other side again. "All I can tell you," he said then, "is that the way the Robinsons travel is like space travel, the actual physical crossing of those enormous distances." He shrugged. "But if they could step through those two feet of wall without harming themselves or the wall—well, that is how we 'travel.' We don't cross space, we avoid it." He smiled. "Draw a breath here—and exhale it on Verna."

I said softly, "And that's how they arrived, isn't it? The people in the picture. You took them there." He nodded, and I said, "Why?"

He shrugged. "If you saw a neighbor's house on fire, would you rescue his family if you could? As many as you could, at least?"

"Yes."

"Well—so would we."

"You think it's that bad, then? With us?"

"How does it look to you?"

I thought about the headlines in my morning paper, that morning and every morning. "Not so good."

He just nodded and said, "We can't take you all, can't even take very many. So we've been selecting a few."

"For how long?"

"A long time." He smiled. "One of us was a member of Lincoln's cabinet. But it was not until just before your First World War that we felt we could see what was coming; until then we'd been merely observers. We opened our first agency in Mexico City in nineteen thirteen. Now we have branches in every major city."

"Nineteen thirteen," I murmured, as something caught at my memory. "Mexico. Listen! Did——"

"Yes." He smiled, anticipating my question. "Ambrose Bierce joined us that year, or the next. He lived until nineteen thirty-one, a very old man, and wrote four more books, which we have." He turned back a page in the folder and pointed to a cabin in the first large photograph. "That was his home."

"And what about Judge Crater?"

"Crater?"

"Another famous disappearance; he was a New York judge who simply disappeared some years ago."

"I don't know. We had a judge, I remember, from New York City, some twenty-odd years ago, but I can't recall his name."

I leaned across the counter toward him, my face very close to his, and I nodded. "I like your little joke," I said. "I like it very much, more than I can possibly tell you." Very softly I added, "When does it stop being a joke?"

For a moment he studied me; then he spoke; "Now. If you want it to."

You've got to decide on the spot, the middle-aged man at the Lexington Avenue bar had told me, *because you'll never get another chance. I know; I've tried.* Now I stood there thinking; there were people I'd hate never to see again, and a girl I was just getting to know, and this was the world I'd been born in. Then I thought about leaving this room, going back to my job, then back to my room at night. And finally I thought of the deep green valley in the picture and the little yellow beach in the morning sun. "I'll go," I whispered. "If you'll have me."

He studied my face. "Be sure," he said sharply. "Be certain. We want no one there who won't be happy, and if you have any least doubt, we'd prefer that—"

"I'm sure," I said.

After a moment the gray-haired man slid open a drawer under the counter and brought out a little rectangle of yellow cardboard. One side was printed, and through the printing ran a band of light green; it looked like a railroad ticket to White Plains or somewhere. The printing said, "Good, when validated, for ONE TRIP TO VERNA. Nontransferable. One way only."

"Ah—how much?" I said, reaching for my wallet, wondering if he wanted me to pay.

He glanced at my hand on my hip pocket. "All you've got. Including your small change." He smiled. "You won't need it any more, and we can use your currency for operating expenses. Light bills, rent, and so on."

"I don't have much."

"That doesn't matter." From under the counter he brought out a heavy stamping machine, the kind you see in railroad ticket offices. "We once sold a ticket for thirty-seven hundred dollars. And we sold another just like it for six cents." He slid the ticket into the machine, struck the lever with his fist, then handed the ticket to me. On the back, now, was a freshly printed rectangle of purple ink, and within it the words, "Good this day only," followed by the date. I put two five-dollar bills, a one, and seventeen cents in change on the counter. "Take the ticket to the Acme Depot," the gray-haired man said, and, leaning across the counter, began giving me directions for getting there.

It's a tiny hole in the wall, the Acme Depot; you may have seen it—just a little store front on one of the narrow streets west of Broadway. On the window is printed, not very well, "Acme." Inside, the walls and ceiling, under layers of old paint, are covered with the kind of stamped tin you see in old buildings. There's a worn wooden counter and a few battered chrome and imitation red leather chairs. There are scores of places like the Acme Depot in that area—little theater-ticket agencies, obscure busline offices, employment agencies. You could pass this one a thousand times and never really see it; and if you live in New York, you probably have.

Behind the counter, when I arrived, stood a shirt-sleeved man, smoking a cigar stump and working on some papers; four or five people silently waited in the chairs. The man at the counter glanced up as I stepped in, looked down at my hand for my ticket, and when I showed it, nodded at the last vacant chair, and I sat down.

There was a girl beside me, hands folded on her purse. She was pleasant-looking, rather pretty; I thought she might have been a stenographer. Across the narrow little office sat a young Negro in work clothes, his wife beside him holding their little girl in her lap. And there was a man of around fifty, his face averted from the rest of us, staring out into the rain at passing pedestrians. He was expensively dressed and wore a gray Homburg; he could have been the vice-president of a large bank, I thought, and I wondered what his ticket had cost.

Maybe twenty minutes passed, the man behind the counter working on his papers; then a small battered old bus pulled up at the curb outside, and I heard the hand brake set. The bus was a shabby thing, bought third- or fourthhand and painted red and white over the old paint, the fenders lumpy from countless pounded-out dents, the tire treads worn almost smooth. On the side, in red letters, it said "Acme," and the driver wore a leather jacket and the kind of worn cloth cap that cab drivers wear. It was precisely the sort of obscure little bus you see around there, ridden always by shabby, tired, silent people, going no one knows where.

It took over an hour for the little bus to work south through the traffic, toward the tip of Manhattan, and we all sat, each wrapped in his own silence and thoughts, staring out the rain-spattered windows; the little girl was asleep. Through the streaking glass beside me I watched drenched people huddled at city bus stops, and saw them rap angrily on the closed doors of buses jammed to capacity, and saw the strained, harassed faces of the drivers. At Fourteenth Street I saw a speeding cab splash a sheet of street-dirty water on a man at the curb, and saw the man's mouth writhe as he cursed. Often our bus stood motionless, the traffic light red, as throngs flowed out into the street from the curb, threading their way around us and the other waiting cars. I saw hundreds of faces, and not once did I see anyone smile.

I dozed; then we were on a glistening black highway somewhere on Long Island. I slept again, and awakened in darkness as we jolted off the highway onto a muddy double-rut road, and I caught a glimpse of a farmhouse, the windows dark. Then the bus slowed, lurched once, and stopped. The hand brake set, the motor died, and we were parked beside what looked like a barn.

It *was* a barn. . . . The driver walked up to it, pulled the big sliding wood door open, its wheels creaking on the rusted old trolley overhead, and stood holding it open as we filed in.

Then he released it, stepping inside with us, and the big door slid closed of its own weight. The barn was damp, old, the walls no longer plumb, and it smelled of cattle; there was nothing inside on the packed-dirt floor but a bench of unpainted pine, and the driver indicated it with the beam of a flashlight. "Sit here, please," he said quietly. "Get your tickets ready." Then he moved down the line, punching each of our tickets, and on the floor I caught a momentary glimpse, in the shifting beam of his light, of tiny mounds of countless more round bits of cardboard, like little drifts of yellow confetti. Then he was at the door again, sliding it open just enough to pass through, and for a moment we saw him silhouetted against the night sky. "Good luck," he said. "Just wait where you are." He released the door; it slid closed, snipping off the wavering beam of his flashlight; and a moment later we heard the motor start and the bus lumber away in low gear.

The dark barn was silent now, except for our breathing. Time ticked away, and I felt an urge, presently, to speak to whoever was next to me. But I didn't quite know what to say, and I began to feel embarrassed, a little foolish, and very aware that I was simply sitting in an old and deserted barn. The seconds passed, and I moved my feet restlessly; presently I realized that I was getting cold and chilled. Then suddenly I knew—and my face flushed in violent anger and a terrible shame. We'd been tricked! Bilked out of our money by our pathetic will to believe an absurd and fantastic fable and left, now, to sit there as long as we pleased, until we came to our senses finally, like countless others before us, and made our way home as best we could. It was suddenly impossible to understand or even remember how I could have been so gullible, and I was on my feet, stumbling through the dark across the uneven floor, with some notion of getting to a phone and the police. The big barn door was heavier than I'd thought, but I slid it back, took a running step through it, then turned to shout back to the others to come along.

You have seen how very much you can observe in the fractional instant of a lightning flash—an entire landscape sometimes, every detail etched on your memory, to be seen and studied in your mind for long moments afterward. As I turned back toward the opened door the inside of that barn came alight. Through every wide crack of its walls and ceiling and through the big dust-coated windows in its side streamed the light of an intensely brilliant blue and sunny sky, and the air pulling into my lungs as I opened my mouth to shout was sweeter than any I had ever tasted in my life. Dimly, through a wide, dust-smeared window of that barn, I looked—for less than the blink of an eye—down into a deep majestic V of forest-covered slope, and I saw, tumbling through it, far below, a tiny stream, blue from the sky, and at that stream's edge between two low roofs a yellow patch of sun-drenched beach. And then, that picture engraved on my mind forever, the heavy door slid shut, my fingernails rasping along the splintery wood in a desperate effort to stop it—and I was standing alone in a cold and rain-swept night.

It took four or five seconds, no longer, fumbling at that door, to heave it open again. But it was four or five seconds too long. The barn was empty, dark. There was nothing inside but a worn pine bench—and, in the flicker of the lighted match in my hand, tiny drifts of what looked like damp confetti on the floor. As my mind had known even as my hands scratched at the outside of that door, there was no one inside now; and I knew where they were—knew they were walking, laughing aloud in a sudden wonderful and eager ecstasy, down into that forest-green valley, toward home.

I work in a bank, in a job I don't like; and I ride to and

from it in the subway, reading the daily papers, the news they contain. I live in a rented room, and in the battered dresser under a pile of my folded handkerchiefs is a little rectangle of yellow cardboard. Printed on its face are the words, "Good, when validated, for one trip to Verna," and stamped on the back is a date. But the date is gone, long since, the ticket void, punched in a pattern of tiny holes.

I've been back to the Acme Travel Bureau. The first time the tall gray-haired man walked up to me and laid two five-dollar bills, a one, and seventeen cents in change before me. "You left this on the counter last time you were here," he said gravely. Looking me squarely in the eyes, he added bleakly, "I don't know why." Then some customers came in, he turned to greet them, and there was nothing for me to do but leave.

Walk in as though it were the ordinary agency it seems—you can find it, somewhere, in any city you try! Ask a few ordinary questions—about a trip you're planning, a vacation, anything you like. Then hint about The Folder a little, but don't mention it directly. Give him time to size you up and offer it himself. And if he does, if you're the type, if you can believe—*then make up your mind and stick to it! Because you won't ever get a second chance. I know, because I've tried. And tried. And tried.*

Lunch-Hour Magic

I'm a big noon-hour prowler. I like to duck out of the office when I haven't a lunch date, grab a fast bite, pick up a Hershey bar or a Snickers or something, and then poke around—into a Second Avenue antique store with a bell that clanks when you open the door, or an unclaimed-parcel auction, a store-front judo school, secondhand bookshop, pinball emporium, pawnshop, fifth-rate hotel lobby—you know what I mean?

You do if you've ever been a noon-hour prowler, but there aren't too many of them, not real ones. The only other one I ever ran into from our office—Simon & Laurentz, an advertising agency on Park near Forty-fourth—was Frieda Piper from the art department. I wandered into a First Avenue hardware store one noon this last May and there she was back in the store fiddling with a lathe. At least I was pretty sure no one else could look quite that shapeless and down-at-the-heels, though it was a little dark in there and her back was to me. But, when she turned at the sound of the door opening and her hair fell over her face, I knew it had to be Frieda.

She wore her hair like someone in an 1895 out-of-focus tintype, parted somewhere near the middle in a jagged lightning streak, hanging straight down at the sides, and snarled up at the back in a sagging granny-knot. It covered the sides of her face as though she were peeking out through a pair of curtains, and it kept creeping out over her eyes as though she'd ducked back behind them. Walking toward her through the hardware store I was thinking that her dresses were like old ladies' hats; you couldn't imagine where they sold that kind. The one she had on now, like all her others, was no particular color; call it anything and you wouldn't be wrong. It was a sort of reddish, greenish, blackish, brownish, haphazard draping of cloth that looked as though it had accidentally fallen on her from a considerable height; even I could see that the hem on one side was a good three inches lower than the other.

The heels of her shoes—not just the ones she had on now but all her shoes all the time—were so run down that her ankles bent out as though she were learning to skate, and her stocking seams were so crooked you wouldn't have been surprised if they'd actually turned loops. It was an office joke that she bought her stockings in special unmatched pairs with the runs already in, and she's the only young adult woman I ever saw with one of the side pieces of her glasses broken and held together with adhesive tape. They were the same kind of fancy glasses other girls wear, studded here and there with little shiny stones, but half the stones were missing, and the glasses were so knocked out of shape that they hung cockeyed on her nose, one eye almost squinting out over the top of the frame, the other trying to peer out underneath. She looked like the model for some of her own wilder cartoons.

I said, "Hi, Frieda; buying a lathe?"

She surprised me. "Hi, Ted," she said. "Yeah, I'm thinking about it. I've got a drill press, a router, a planer, a belt-sander, and a nine-inch table saw; now I need a lathe." I looked puzzled; someone had told me she lived in a little two-room apartment on upper Madison Avenue somewhere. She said, "Oh, I haven't much room to use them, but I'm crazy about tools! I'm not too interested in clothes," she said as though she thought I might not have noticed, "so I'm filling my hope chest with tools. Some day when I'm married, I can build all our furniture. Maybe even the house."

I was pleased at the thought of a girl with a hope chest full of power tools, and wanted to hear a little more about it, and I brought out a Baby Ruth I'd bought, and offered Frieda some. She said no, she still had half a Love Nest left, and pulled it out of her skirt pocket, and we wandered around the hardware store for a while. She chattered away about her wood-working projects. One of them, a wedding gift for her future husband, was to be an enormous multiple-dwelling birdhouse, a sort of slum-clearance project I gathered, and I figured that the guy who married her would probably appreciate it.

She talked all the way back to the office, looking up at me eagerly through her slanted glasses, shoving the hair back off her face. The upper edge of her glasses bisected her right eye, the lower edge bisected the left; and since one lens made half her eye slightly smaller than normal, while the other lens magnified half of the remaining eye, she seemed to have four separate half-eyes of varying sizes, resembling a Picasso painting, and I got a little dizzy and tripped and nearly fell over a curb.

But I learned that Frieda was a full-fledged noon-hour prowler; she'd been to most of the places I had, and she mentioned several, including a bootleg tattooing parlor in the back of a cut-rate undertaker's place, that I hadn't run across. So I wasn't surprised later that week when I passed a Lexington Avenue dance studio to see Frieda there. It was on the second floor, a corner room with big windows; I'd stopped in one noon and knew they offered you a free trial lesson when you came in. So now as I passed on the opposite side of the street, I glanced up and there was Frieda taking the free lesson, her dress billowing and flapping like loose sails in a typhoon. Her head rested dreamily on the instructor's shoulder, her eyes were closed behind the cockeyed glasses, and she was chewing in time to the music; the hand behind the instructor's back held half a candy bar. He was looking down at her as though he were wondering how he'd ever gotten into this line of work.

The reason I mention Frieda is because of what happened the following week. One noon hour I was clear across town wandering around west of Sixth Avenue in the Forties somewhere, and I came to a narrow little place jammed in between an all-night barbershop and a Turkish bath. It said MAGIC SHOP on the window, and down in a corner in smaller letters, NOVELTIES, JOKES, JEWELRY, SOUVENIRS. I went in, of course; there were glass showcases on three sides, practically filling the place. The proprietor was back of one, leaning on the counter reading the *Daily News*. He was a thin, tired-looking, bald guy about thirty-five, and he just looked up and nodded, then went back to his paper till I was ready for business.

I looked at the stuff in the showcases; it was about what you'd expect. There was some jewelry in one case—fake gold rings mounted with big zircons, imitation turquoise-and-silver Navaho jewelry, Chinese good-luck rings. On one counter was a metal rack filled with printed comic signs, and a display of practical jokes in the showcase underneath; a plastic ice cube with a fly in it; an ink bottle with a shiny metal puddle of what looked like spilled ink—that kind of stuff. I said, "What's new in the magic-trick line?" and the guy finished a line of what he was reading, then looked up.

"Well," he said, "have you seen this?" and reached into the showcase and brought out a little brass cylinder with a handle, but I recognized it. It changed a little stack of nickels into dimes, and I told him I'd seen it. "Well, there's this," he said, and brought out a trick deck of cards, and demonstrated them, staring boredly out the window as he shuffled. I nodded when he finished, and waited. For a moment he stood thinking, then he shrugged a little, reached into the showcase, and pulled out a cheap gray cardboard box filled with a dozen or so pairs of glasses. "These are new; some salesman left them last week." I picked up a pair, and looked at them; it was just a cheap plastic frame with clear-glass lenses, no false nose attached or anything like that, and I looked up at the guy again, and said, "What're they for?"

He reached wearily into the showcase once more—he'd demonstrated so many little tricks for so many people and made so few sales—and brought out a thin silk handkerchief. He made a fist with his other hand, draped the handkerchief over it, and held it up. "Put on the glasses," he said, and I did.

It wasn't a bad trick. As soon as I put on the glasses I could see his fist under the handkerchief very clearly, the handkerchief itself barely visible. "Not bad," I said, "How's it work?"

He shrugged. "I don't know. Salesman said a few rays of light get through cloth if it's thin, but not enough to see by. The lenses are ground some way to magnify the rays so you can see the hand underneath."

I nodded, taking the glasses off to examine them. "Is that the whole trick?"

"Yeah." He looked away boredly. "There are a couple others you can do with it, too."

I glanced out the window. A truck and several cabs stood motionless, blocked in a traffic jam. A man in a business suit and carrying a briefcase turned to cross the street between two of the cabs. A tall good-looking showgirl type from one of the theaters around here walked along the other side of the street. I put the glasses on again absently, wondering if I wanted them; I felt I ought to buy something. The truck and the cabs sat there, the drivers leaning on their wheels trying to keep calm. The man in the business suit stepped up onto the opposite curb. The showgirl was still walking—the showgirl's *dress* was gone!

There she was, walking along just as before glancing into store windows, and wearing nothing but high heels, a bra, lace-edged panties, and a purse! Then I saw the dress, ghostlike and almost invisible, swaying as she walked. I snatched off the glasses, and instantly the dress was solid—thin but nontransparent cloth. I jammed the glasses back on before she got out of sight, almost putting my eye out with one of the side pieces, the dress became ghostly, and there she was again, by George, that handsome swaying figure under the nearly vanished dress marvelously visible once more.

I rushed to the doorway, looked toward the corner, and there they all were—all the sweet young office girls, not in their summer dresses but walking delightfully along in shoes, bras, and panties. It was entrancing, and I stood there for several happy and amazing minutes. When I finally turned back into the store again the proprietor was reading the *News*. "Ah, look," I said, hesitating, "these are fine, but . . . I was wondering if you had a stronger pair?"

He shook his head. "No, but it's funny, that's something I get a lot of calls for, and I'm going to check the salesman next time he comes in. These only work through one or two layers of pretty thin cloth; not much use for anything but tricks, far as I can see. There's a couple of good ones, though. For example, you have someone wrap a coin in a handker—"

"Yeah, yeah; how much?"

"Buck and a quarter plus tax," he said, and I bought them, and walked back to the office—strolled, actually, and it was wonderful. It was absolutely fascinating, in fact, and it seems to me that if girls understood how delicious they look walking along as I saw them now, they'd dress that way all the time, at least in nice weather. It'd be a lot cooler, terrifically healthy, and would bring a great deal of happiness into a drab prosaic world. It might even bring about world peace; it's worth trying anyway.

I sauntered along observing, and grinning so happily—I couldn't help it—that people began staring at me wonderingly, girls especially. Once, stopped on a corner waiting for the traffic cop to wave us across, I stood beside a very good-looking girl with a haughty face—the kind that shrivels you with a look if you so much as glance at her. She stood there in—I don't know why, but it's true—a bright blue bra and a pair of vivid orange panties; I noticed that she was slightly knock-kneed. I leaned toward her, and murmured very quietly, "Orange and blue don't go together." She looked at me puzzledly, then her eyes suddenly widened, and she stared at me with her mouth opening. Then she whirled and began looking frantically around her. The light changed, the cop waving us across, and she headed out into the street toward him, and I ran across to the other curb, glancing at my watch so people would think I'd suddenly remembered I was late somewhere. Then I ducked into a building lobby across the street, snatching off the glasses so I'd be harder to identify, and just as I yanked them off I passed a girl who wasn't even wear—but I didn't stop; I hurried on, and came out of the building a block away just across the street from my office.

Upstairs in the office, Zoe was at the switchboard in the lobby as I came in. She was the best-looking girl in the office, resembling Anita Ekberg, only slimmer—more of a fashion-model type. I whipped out my glasses, put them on, said, "Hi," smiling at her as I passed, and—what a disappointment! There under that expensive, smart-looking, narrow-waisted, flounced-out dress sat a girl only ounces this side of malnutrition. It was the kind of figure that women, in their pitiful ignorance, envy; no hips, no nothing, except prominent ribs. "You don't eat enough, Zoe," I said.

She nodded proudly. "That's what my roommate says."

"Well, he's right."

"Listen, wise guy," she began, and I held up a hand placatingly, ducking behind one shoulder, and she smiled, and I walked on.

I kept the glasses on nearly all afternoon, wandering around the office with a sheaf of papers in my hand, and strangely it was Mrs. Humphrey, our middle-aged overweight bookkeeper, that I stared at longest. Last year, I knew, she'd celebrated the twenty-fifth anniversary of her marriage to her husband, Harvey. But there, unmistakably, tattooed on her left hip, was a four-inch-high red heart inside which, in a slanted blue script, was inscribed *Ralph,* and I wondered if she'd had the fearsome job of hiding it from Harvey for a quarter of a century.

But the biggest surprise of all came just before quitting time. I was managing to do a little actual work by then, and, when my office door opened and someone came in, I raised my eyes slowly, still reading a last few words of the paper in my hand. And there before me in bra and what I believe are called briefs embroidered with forget-me-nots, and I swore I never would, was—well, there is no describing what I saw, and I'm not going to try. It was nothing more or less than the most magnificently beautiful feminine figure the human race has ever known. It may even have been a mutant figure, the very first example of a new height in beauty to which humanity has never previously soared. I couldn't believe it, I couldn't tear away my eyes and lift my head until, entranced with those flawless beautifully shaped long legs, something vaguely familiar began tapping at the doors of my flabbergasted memory. The ankles, I saw when I reached them, were strangely bowed out, and then my chin shot up and I was staring openmouthed at the face above that incredible figure. "Did I startle you or something, Ted? Sorry," said Frieda, raking back a dank curtain of hair to expose a constellation of half-eyes of various sizes blinking down at me from behind and around those demented glasses.

"That's all right," I managed to say. "I've been concentrating all afternoon on some figures." I yanked off my glasses, and sure enough, there stood Frieda as always—in a shapeless sackcloth, which the dictionary says is made of goat's or camel's hair, and in her case I didn't doubt it.

"Forgot to tell you," she said, "that I found a ladies' pool hall on Sixth Avenue last month," and I thanked her, and she left. I couldn't quite believe what had happened and I clapped my glasses on again and stared after her. But it was true. There, wobbling along on scuffed and run-down heels, went the world's greatest figure, and I pulled off my glasses, and sat there till quitting time rubbing the corners of my eyes between my thumb and forefinger.

I soon quit wearing my glasses regularly though I kept them in the breast pocket of my coat for emergency use. But the novelty of wearing them all the time wore off quickly; it was like walking around on a beach all day, you got used to it. And I never put them on—the contrast between face and figure was just too much—when Frieda dropped into my office as she took to doing. She'd stop in to tell me about some noon-hour discovery, and I told her about the magic shop and about a jail manufacturer on lower Park Avenue. Usually she'd be eating a Love Nest candy bar, not so much because of the taste, she explained, but because she loved to ask for them.

Coming to work on the Forty-ninth Street crosstown bus one morning about a week later, I sat down next to the optometrist in our building; his shop is in the lobby, he usually stands in the doorway between customers, and we generally nod and speak, so I knew him. We spoke now, then each sat reading our papers till the bus stopped for a light. I looked up to see where we were just as a particularly extravagant example of lush American girlhood was crossing the street, and I whipped out my glasses and clapped them on in a blur of movement; I now had, I felt sure, the fastest draw in the East. "Farsighted?" my optometrist friend asked me, and I said no, these lenses were ground so you could see through thin cloth, such as summer dresses. He chuckled delightedly, and said, "Any lenses that could do that must be magic." I snatched off the glasses, and stared at him.

"You mean you couldn't make lenses like that?" I said finally.

"Of course not," he said with the tolerant little chuckle doctors use for the idiot questions of stupid laymen. The bus was slowing for Park Avenue, and he stood up, asking me if I weren't going to get off, but I shook my head.

"There's something I've got to do near Sixth Avenue; I just realized," I said, and rode on across town.

The guy in the magic shop looked up from his *Daily News* as I walked in, and shook his head. "That salesman was in again but he doesn't have any stronger glasses; I asked."

"Never mind, that's not why I came," I said. "Tell me; what does this salesman look like? Does he have a thin saturnine face, a little waxed mustache, and strangely hypnotic eyes? Is his hair black and glossy, and high above the temples as though concealing little horns? Does he wear a silk hat and a full dress suit, and is there an odor of brimstone about h—"

"No, you must be thinking of a salesman for some other company. This here salesman is fat. Wears dirty wash pants, a Hawaiian shirt, and a cap. Smokes a cigar that smells a little like brimstone, though."

I nodded, disappointed, then thought of something. "He was here again, did you say? What'd he leave this time?"

"Some lousy jewelry. Cheap plated brass. I wouldn't of took it if he didn't leave it on consignment."

I shrugged. "Might as well look at it, long as I'm here."

"Help yourself." He pulled a cardboard box out of a showcase, shoved it across the counter at me, and went back to the *News*. Tumbled in the box lay a dozen or so heart-shaped little boxes made of cheap pink plastic. I opened one; a layer of pink imitation felt was glued to a piece of cardboard cut to fit the inside of the box. Lying on the felt was a bracelet of imitation brass chain studded with red glass hearts; it was as gaudy a looking thing as I'd seen in a long time. A badly printed label stuck to the inside of the lid read, GENUINE EGYPTIAN SLAVE BRACELET, and a little gummed tab on the back said 75¢. I paid the guy—he looked at me pityingly as I did—then hurried out and to the office.

Zoe was at the switchboard, looking—with clothes on—as lovely as ever, and I stopped; there was no one else around. I took out the little pink box, opened it, and showed her the bracelet. "Just bought this," I said.

She glanced at the bracelet, then up at me. "Bought it? Or did you find it in a box of Crackerjack?"

"Bought it. Try it on; I'd like to see how it looks."

She frowned but picked up the bracelet, slipped it over her

wrist, then held out her arm to inspect the result; it looked terrible. I said, "Zoe, you are now my slave; kiss me, you mad fool!" and she stood up, walked out of her little enclosure, grabbed me around the waist, bent me far back—it was like a reverse scene from a Rudolph Valentino movie—stared into my eyes for a moment, then kissed me. Enormous blue sparks flashed and crackled around the room like St. Elmo's fire; it was the most wildly abandoned and passionate kiss I'd ever imagined, and I've imagined some beauties.

It didn't stop, either. Behind us the switchboard buzzed, then another buzz began in a slightly different key, then a third. But I didn't realize it was the switchboard; I thought it was my nerves twanging in ecstasy and my mind and senses threw up their hands and went down for the first, then the second time, and were just going under for the third when I managed to reach out with my little remaining strength and yank the bracelet off her wrist or there's simply no telling what might have happened. Zoe raised her lovely head, stared down at me for a moment, said, "For heaven's sakes," and let me drop to run for her board. I fell flat on my back, banging my head on the floor, and raising a considerable lump. Then I hurried on, fifteen minutes late for work, as Zoe began clearing her board of calls, murmuring, "Sorry!"

In my office I closed the door, sat down at my desk, and with trembling hands began putting the bracelet back into its box. The door opened, and Frieda walked in saying, "Did you know there's a blacksmith shop down on Twenty-eighth Str—" Then she stopped, her mouth still open, and stood staring down at the bracelet in the pink heart-shaped box. She leaned closer, her hair fell over her face, and with both hands she pulled it aside like Stanley parting the jungle vines. For a moment longer she stared, then said, "Isn't it *beautiful!* Oh, Ted, it's the loveliest thing I've ever seen!"

I looked at her quickly but she wasn't kidding. Her eyes, face, and voice were filled with the kind of yearning the Little Match Girl might feel gazing through the store window at the doll she could never have, and I realized that Frieda was probably the only human being in the civilized world who could think that damn bracelet was beautiful. I knew I could get another at noon, so I said, "You like it? It's yours," and handed it to her box and all. I was glad I did, because Frieda was entranced. Thanking me again and again, she put it on, then stood revolving her wrist so the bracelet would catch the light till I thought her arm would fall off.

That noon I stood in the magic shop, and I couldn't believe—my mind wouldn't accept—what the man was telling me. But he repeated it. "That's right; a guy bought one right after you left this morning, and half an hour later he came back for the rest. Wanted to buy a gross, but I didn't have them."

I could hardly speak. "But . . . can't you get more?"

He shrugged, turning a page of the *News*. "I'll try. I'll ask the salesman next time he comes around. But he don't ever seem to have the same thing twice. Tried to get more of those glasses, but couldn't. Seems like he's more interested pushing new items than repeats."

I didn't eat lunch; I didn't feel like it. I bought an Almond Joy, but could only eat half. And when, wandering aimlessly around, I passed an embalming school, I didn't even bother reading the placard in the window.

Back at the office I felt even worse, because in came Frieda to thank me again, holding her arm up so I could admire the bracelet. I sat looking at it and thinking that this was typical of me; here was the only genuine Egyptian slave bracelet, I knew now, that I'd ever get my hands on, and of all the wrists of all the girls in the world I'd somehow managed to get it onto Frieda's. Looking at it as her wrist twisted and flashed like the revolving red light on top of a cop's car, I thought of what might have been.

I pictured myself going to Hollywood; I'd have had to travel by bus, eating almost nothing, but I could have managed it, and it would have been worth it. Somehow, I knew, I could have gotten into the studio, found Anita Ekberg, and when she wasn't looking, slipped the bracelet onto her magnificent wrist, and then—but I couldn't bear to finish that lovely dream, not with Frieda standing there wearing the bracelet, yakking away about it and smiling down at me from behind and around those insane glasses.

Twice I opened my mouth to tell her that I had to have that bracelet back, that it was a family heirloom and that I'd get her another that was bigger, better, and even gaudier. But I simply could not get the words out; I just couldn't do it. Could you take a big delicious piece of candy away from a child, telling her you'd get her a better one some other time? It just wasn't possible to take that bracelet away, yet the thought of a genuine slave bracelet being entirely wasted was more than I could stand. It was too much to bear, and I had a sudden idea.

I took out my glasses, put them on, and then—careful not to lift my eyes too high and catch sight of her face—I slowly looked up at Frieda. The embroidered forget-me-nots were gone today but I hadn't forgotten; there beside my desk, ankles bowed outward and one wrist steadily revolving, stood the world's most spectacular figure. And now, by an inspired act of will, keeping my eyes carefully lowered, I pictured Zoe's lovely face at the upper end of that splendid torso. It was a spectacular combination, and I stood up saying, "Kiss me; you are my slave," and she did, her arms winding immediately around my neck.

It was great! It was wonderful! And when we finally stopped, Frieda sighed deeply and said, "Do you always put on your glasses to kiss a girl?" I said yeah, and she said, "Then why are your eyes closed?"

"Shut up and kiss me again," I said and she did and this time it lasted even longer and was tremendous. Just kiss a girl like Zoe some time with your arms around a figure like that, and you'll know what I mean. It was so great, in fact, that the actual truth of what was happening faded from my mind. In a fit of delirious absentmindedness I languorously opened my eyes, and there only half an inch away and staring into mine were Frieda's eyes—all of them. I got so dizzy I had to break loose and sit down on the edge of the desk; not because of the split-level eyes in assorted sizes—I was used to them now—but because every single one of them was chock full of love. They were filled with it! They swam with it! And from an enormous distance I heard Frieda saying, "Oh, Ted, darling, you're wonderful! I love you! Open your eyes!"

I couldn't; I'd closed them again instantly and they were squeezed tight as though I had soap in them. Then I forced myself; cautiously opening my eyes to a slit I looked again. They were still there in front of me, those four half-eyes each aflame with the light of love, and I slammed my eyelids shut knowing that, although it hardly seemed possible, I'd managed to make things infinitely worse. "I'm crazy about you, Ted!" Frieda was saying. "I'm your slave!" She reached out and pulled off my glasses saying, "Please open your eyes and kiss me again!"

Bravely, I looked out once more; she was peering tenderly out at me from behind that jungle of hair looking as though she'd just jumped from a plane in a burlap parachute in which she'd become hopelessly tangled. I thought of pretending to faint, when my phone rang and I snatched it up before the first ring had stopped. It was just one of the account men with one of the foolish questions they ask, and which I answered with a word. But I kept the phone at my ear long after he'd hung up, saying, "Yeah," and "You bet," over and over again, occasionally looking up at Frieda and shrugging helplessly. Finally she had to leave, giggling and murmuring horrible endearments, and I hung up the phone, covered my face with my hands, and planted my elbows on the desk squarely on the glasses Frieda had put there, smashing both lenses, but I was beyond caring.

Later, splashing cold water on my face in the washroom, I wondered what to do. Here was a girl helplessly in love with me and it was all my fault; maybe I was morally obliged to pretend that I, too—but I knew I couldn't do that. I went back to my desk, and three times that afternoon Frieda looked in hopefully, lovingly, and I told her that I had a headache. At quitting time I found her waiting at the elevators, and told her my headache was far worse and by this time it was true; it throbbed and pounded, and I stumbled home to a night of hideous dreams.

I don't know whether Frieda guessed the truth that night; I'm just not sure. But all next morning she didn't come into my office, though I kept glancing up every time footsteps sounded anywhere near my door. When noon came and she still hadn't come in, I was suddenly filled with remorse and fear. This was a nice girl, I'd probably hurt her feelings terribly, and—what if she were at the river, *in* it by now going down for the last time, refusing to struggle? All noon hour I prowled along the river front cursing myself, worrying, and when I got back to the office, and sat down at my desk, and Frieda came in friendly and happy as ever, I jumped up and yelled, "Where *were* you this noon!?"

She just smiled, and shook her head. "Want some?" she

said, holding out a wrapped candy bar clutched in her hand like a banana; but printed on the wrapper just above her fist I could see the first word, Love, and the beginning vertical stroke of the next, and since Love Nests aren't really my favorite, I said no, thanks. But when she peeled off the wrapper, and urged me again, it occurred to me that I could hardly be expected to kiss her with my mouth full of candy, so I took a bite. Surprisingly, it was delicious, and when she offered me some more, I took another. Her eyes gleaming with love, she said, "Finish it," insisting with a gesture, so I did—chewing slowly, postponing as long as possible what I was afraid would happen next.

It happened. "Kiss me, lover," Frieda said then, and I looked up at her, my mouth opening to say that my headache was back. But I didn't say it. My mouth stayed open but I just sat looking at her astounded. It had suddenly occurred to me that if Frieda would simply use a judicious bobby pin or two and unsnarl that knot at the back, her hair would not only stay in place but would become a very handsome pageboy bob. And that if she'd just take off those crazy—I stood up as though in a dream, and did it myself. I pulled off those nutty glasses, and her various half-eyes merged in pairs like the split images in a camera viewfinder coming into focus, and turned into a single set of enormous, beautiful, myopic blue eyes. She couldn't see me now but I could see her, and her face was absolutely lovely, every bit as beautiful as the accompanying figure which I now found I was holding in my arms. I started to say something about contact lenses but decided that could wait while this could not—and I kissed her long and lingeringly.

For a moment I drew back to look down at that wonderful face, then grabbed her to me again, murmuring all sorts of trite phrases such as "I love you," to which Frieda said, "Of course," and, "When can we get married?" to which she said, "As soon as I finish your birdhouse." Looking down over her lovely shoulder, I noticed the candy wrapper lying where she'd dropped it on my desk, and now I could read both the words printed on it. Love Potion, they said in big blue letters and now I knew where Frieda had been during noon hour.

Where the Cluetts Are

We had open books and magazines lying on every flat surface in the room. They stood propped in a row along the fireplace mantel and lay face up on the seat cushions of the upholstered chairs. They hung like little tents on the chair arms and backs, were piled in layers on the big round coffee table, and lay scattered all over the carpeted floor. Every one of them was opened to a photograph, sketch, floor plan, or architect's elevation of a house. Ellie Cluett sat on the top of the ladder I used to reach the highest of the bookshelves. She was wearing a gray sweater and slacks and was slowly leafing through an *Architectural Forum*. Sam, her husband, sat on the floor, his back against the bookshelves, and now he held up his book for us to look at. This was the big room I worked in and I was at my drafting table watching them.

"How about something like this?" Sam said. It was a color photograph of the Taj Mahal.

Ellie said, "Great. The big dome in the center is just right for a television aerial. Okay with you, Harry?"

"Sure. All I have to do is design the place. You'll have to

live in it." I smiled at Ellie. She was about twenty-three, intelligent and likable.

Sam said, "Well, I wish you *would* design it and quit pestering us about it." He grinned to show he didn't mean it, though he did. Sam was wearing slacks and a sports shirt and was about my age—somewhere just over thirty.

Ellie said, "Yes, Harry, please. Have it built, and phone us in New York when it's finished. Surprise us! Honestly"—she gestured at the roomful of opened books and magazines—"I know we promised to look through all this, but it's driving me crazy."

"I'll have the rooms padded, then. In tasteful decorator colors."

"Damn it, Harry, I think you're being pointlessly stubborn," Sam said. "There are only two things that matter to me about this house, and you know what they are."

I nodded. Sam owned a big boatyard on the Sound. He wanted a house here in Darley, Connecticut, because it was only thirty minutes from the yard. He sold his boats by demonstration and entertainment, so he wanted an impressive house to take his prospects to.

Sam said, "That's all I care about, and you won't change it if you lock me up in here."

"It isn't as though we'd really be living here," Ellie said gently. "We'll keep our apartment in New York, you can be sure. Except for the boat season, we'll hardly be in Darley."

I didn't want to lose this job. Just before the boat craze began, Sam Cluett started his boat works on nothing; now he was rich and offering me a free hand in designing a show place with nothing skimped. I wanted to do it and needed the money but I said, "I can't do it alone. If this house doesn't mean enough to you to give it some time and work and to develop some opinions and enthusiasms about it, then I don't want to design it. Because it would never be much of a house. It wouldn't be yours, mine, or anyone's. It would be a house without life or soul—or, even worse, the wrong kind of soul."

Absolutely identical looks came to their faces: brows raised in polite question, eyes alertly interested in and amused by the notion of a house with a soul.

I suspected that I was about to become an anecdote back in New York but I was going to save this job if I could and I smiled and said, "It's true, or close to it. A house can have a life and soul of its own. There's a house here in Darley, twelve years old and it's had nineteen owners. No one ever lives in it long. There are houses like it in every town in the world." I stood up and began walking around the room, hands shoved into my back pockets, picking my way through the scattered books.

Sam sat watching me from the floor, arms folded. Ellie sat on top of the ladder staring down at me, her chin on her fist. There was a faint smile of interest on each face and they looked like a couple of sophisticated kids waiting for the rest of a story.

I said, "It's an ordinary enough house but I prowled through it between tenants, once, and began to understand why it never kept an owner. Everywhere you look the proportions are just faintly unpleasant. There's a feeling of harshness to the place. There's even something wrong in the very way the light slants in through the windows. It wasn't the designer's fault; the house simply developed an ugly life and soul of its own. It's filled with unpleasant associations and after you're in it awhile it becomes downright repelling. I don't really understand why, and I'm an architect." I glanced at Sam, then at Ellie, smiling so as not to seem too deadly serious. Ellie's eyes were bright with interest. I said, "There's another house in Darley that no one has ever willingly left. Those who've left it, the husbands were transferred or something of that sort, and I've heard that each wife cried when she had to give up that house. And that a child in one family said and has continued to say that when he grows up, he's going to buy that house back and live in it. I don't doubt these stories because I've been in that house, too, and I swear it welcomes you as you step through the front door."

I looked at the Cluetts again, and began to hope. I said, "You've been in that kind of house; everyone has. For no reason you can explain you feel a joy at just being in it. I almost think that kind of house *knows* you're in it and puts its best foot forward. There's a kind of felicity about it, everything in it just right. It's something more and better than any designer could consciously plan. It's the occasional rare and wonderful house that somehow acquires a life and soul of its own, and a fine one. Personally, I believe that kind of house comes out of the feelings and attitude and actual love for it of the people who plan it and bring it to life. And that has to be the people who are going to live in it, not just the architect. When I design a house I want it to have a chance of turning out to be that kind. But you're not giving yours any chance at all."

It didn't work. For half an hour, the Cluetts were contrite and industrious, searching through my books and magazines, pointing out to me and each other houses, rooms, windows, doors, roof styles, bathrooms, and gardens they liked or said they did. I sat at my table again, listening, but I knew their interest was synthetic and I added no more notes to the pad in my clip board. I had only one: "Enormous master bdrm w. fireplace." But every client says that; I could have it printed on my note pads. And the Cluetts had nothing more to add, they really didn't care.

Finally, Ellie put a book back on the shelf beside her, then stood up on the ladder and began scanning the top shelf boredly. She reminded me of a child reluctantly doing homework, ready to welcome any diversion, and now she found one. Pulling out a book, she dislodged a thick wadding of paper crammed onto the shelf beside it and caught it as it fell. She unfolded it, opening it up finally to half a dozen big sheets of linen drawing paper each the size of a newspaper page. When she saw what was on the top sheet she slowly sat down on the ladder top, staring and murmuring, "For heaven's sake." After a moment she looked at me, saying, "Harry! What in the world is this?"

"Just what it looks like." I heard the tired irritation in my voice and forced it out before I continued. I wasn't going to take their job, but I liked the Cluetts just the same. "Those are drawings for a house, architectural drawings," I said more pleasantly. "That top sheet is a perspective showing what it would look like finished. The sheets underneath are the working drawings for building it. They've always been up there; belonged to my grandfather. Most of the stuff on that top shelf was his. He was an architect and so was my father."

Sam was getting to his feet, pleased with the diversion, too, and Ellie quickly turned on the ladder, hurried down it, then dropped, kneeling, to the floor and smoothed the big top sheet flat on the rug. "Look!" she said excitedly.

Sam and I went to stand beside her, staring. The edges of the paper were yellowed but the rest was bone-white still and I remembered that I'd once meant to frame this and hang it in my office downtown. It was an India-ink drawing, the lines thin, sharp, and black in the scribed and ruled precision architects once favored. It was an incredible sight—I'd almost forgotten—but there lay the clear sharp-etched architectural rendering for a house of the early 1880s just as its designer had conceived it in every gabled, turreted, dormered, bay-windowed and gingerbreaded detail.

"Imagine," Ellie murmured, her voice incredulous and delighted. "Why, it never entered my head that these houses were actually built!"

"What do you mean?" Sam said.

She turned to look up at him, eyes shining. "Why, they've always *been* here—forever! Since long before any of us was born. They're old, shabby, half tumbling down. It simply never occurred to me that they could ever have been new! Or not even *built* yet, like this one!" Quickly, she began spreading out the other sheets in a half circle.

I knew what she meant and so did Sam, and he nodded. It was strange to see at our feet the actual floor by floor plans—the framing plans and sections, full-sized profiles, every last detail, all precisely dimensioned ready for construction—of what had to seem to our eyes like an old old house. And for some moments, then, silent and bemused, we looked at the careful old drawings thinking the wordless thoughts you often think looking at a relic of other earlier lives than your own.

It seems to me that it's usually impossible to get hold of another time. You look at a pair of high-button shoes, the leather dry and cracked, buttons missing, the cloth uppers nearly drained of color by the years, and it just isn't possible to get into the mind of some long-gone woman who once saw them new. How could they ever have been new and shining, something a woman might actually covet?

But these old drawings lying on the floor beside us weren't quite like any other relic of the past I'd ever before encountered. Because these were the house before it was built; old though they were, these were still the plans for a house-yet-to-be. And so at one and the same time they were quaint and old-fashioned, yet new and fresh, still untouched by the years.

And it was possible to see in them, and feel, not merely quaintness but something of the fresh beauty the architect must have seen and felt the day he finished them a lifetime ago.

Ellie was getting to her feet and I turned to look at her. Her jaw actually hung open a little and her eyes were wide and almost stunned in a kind of incredulous awe at what she'd just thought of. "Sam!" she said, and grabbed his forearm. "Let's build it!"

"What?"

"Yes! I mean it! Let's build it! And I'll furnish it! In the style of those days! Why, good lord," she murmured, turning to stare at nothing, eyes shining with excitement, "there's not a woman I know who won't envy me green."

Sam is bright and used to making decisions, I suppose. His eyes narrowed and he stared at Ellie's face as though testing or absorbing her feelings through her eyes as she stared back at him, elated. Then he stepped forward abruptly and looked down at the drawings again for half a minute. He took a few paces around the room, then turned to me. "Is it possible, Harry? Could that house be built today? Is it practical, I mean? Could we live in it and have it make any kind of sense?" Suddenly he grinned, delighted at the notion.

I shrugged and said, "Sure. Why not? If you're willing to pay the cost. The plans are there and can be followed today as well as in the eighteen eighties." Both started to speak but I held up a hand, cutting them off. "But to build even a contemporary house with that much floor space would be very expensive, Sam. And with this house, every foot of that space would cost twice as much, three times as much, maybe more. Who can say? You might not even get a bid on a job like that."

"Oh? Why not?"

I touched the plans with the toe of my shoe. "Look at the lumber specifications. Half of it different from anything milled today—heavier, thicker, longer. You'd pay a fortune in special milling costs alone. Look at the fancy trim all over the house inside and out. When those plans were drawn I suppose it could be bought from stock. Today it doesn't exist. All of it would have to be special order, lathed and jigsawed out and by people not used to it. Lot of errors and spoilage. What's more, the entire construction method is different from today's. No contractor has had any experience at it, or his men, either. He might not even bid; you'd have to pay cost plus. And the final price?" I shook my head. "It would be fantastic, and if you ever wanted to sell you'd have the world's biggest white elephant on your hands, a brand-new antique that no bank in the world would ever lend you a dime . . ."

Sam shut me off with a hand on my arm, smiling. He said gently, "Everything you're telling me, Harry, can be said in one word—money. Well, I've got the money and whatever it costs to build this house I guarantee you it'll be worth it." He saw I didn't know what he meant, and said, "Harry, boats are sold just like anything else—in a variety of ways. And one of the best ways is publicity. Think of the *talk* this'll make!" He grinned tensely. "Every customer I bring into that house will go home full of it. Why, Sam Cluett's new place will be talked about at cocktail parties, in restaurants, on boat decks, and in living rooms all over the Eastern seaboard. And who is Sam Cluett? Why, he makes boats! Harry, I could blow the place up two years after it's finished and it'll have paid for itself three times over." He turned to Ellie, saying, "Baby, you've picked yourself a house," then he swung back to me. "You know the contractors here. Hire one, Harry, and follow through for me, will you? Don't even ask for a bid; just have him follow the plans and send me his bills as he gets them, adding—what? Twenty per cent? Work it out with him." Sam glanced at his watch. "Now, let's get out of here and go look for a site!"

He was right about the talk. He and Ellie picked a building site that same afternoon, Sunday, and Monday morning I bought it for them—a three-and-a-half-acre plot over three hundred feet deep in the best residential section of town. It had been held for years in the hope of a fat price, and now Sam paid it. And less than seventy-two hours after Ellie Cluett dislodged the papers that were the forgotten plans for a forgotten house, its foundation was being laid—of brick, just as the old plans specified.

At first the new house attracted no attention; the wood frame of one house looks just about like any other at the beginning. Then the roof framing began and before it was finished it was plain to everyone passing that these were remarkably steep and complex gables. They intersected in dozens of places; they were pierced by innumerable dormers; at corners, they rose into sharp, narrow peaks, and they projected over—it was suddenly obvious—what were going to become bay windows and an enormous porch. And now all day every day cars crept past and clusters stood on the sidewalk as people watched the steady, skeletal growth in fresh white pine of a brand-new Victorian mansion.

I was just as fascinated. I had plenty of work. Specifying, ordering, and checking up on all the special milling were a job in themselves and I had much more to do. But still I spent more time at the new house than I really had to. Even at night, as though I were the actual architect, I'd sometimes drive over and prowl around and through it. One night I found Ellie standing on the walk, the big collar of her camel's-hair coat turned up, hands deep in her pockets, looking at the half-finished house.

The house was set far back from the street, and from the sidewalk the eye could take it all in. There was a three-quarter moon; we could see clearly. The new wood looked pale against the night sky and the door and window openings were narrow black rectangles, for the house was no longer skeletal. Most of the exterior sheathing was on, and the external shape of the house was complete. For the first time we could see, rising from the bare wood-littered earth, the beginning reality of what had been only architectural drawings.

Ellie murmured, "Isn't it astonishing?"

"Yeah." I was enjoying the almost ghostly sight of this strange unfinished house in the moonlight and I began fooling, playing with words. "We're looking at a vanished sight. This is a commonplace sight of a world long gone and we've reached back and brought it to life again. Maybe we should have let it alone."

Ellie smiled. "I don't think so. I feel good about it."

The work went fast; the men liked this job. Several had grown mustaches or sideburns in styles they thought appropriate to the house. One of the carpenters had just finished a year in New Jersey doing nothing but hanging doors in over nine hundred identical tract houses. He told me this job was the first time carpentering actually was what, as a boy, he'd imagined it to be. Now the siding was on, and the big veranda was complete. All windows were in. Everything was finished outside, in fact, except the eave ornamentation, not yet delivered, and some special-patterned shingle work on the gable ends.

Inside the hammering was constant—inlaid hardwood floors going down on the third floor, interior trim on the first and second. Plastering was finished, complete with old-style wood lathing, and on the first floor, doors were being hung—inches wider, two feet taller, and far heavier and more solid than any ordinarily made today. Their surfaces were beautifully paneled with fine moldings, and they, too, were new-minted and fresh-sanded, not even drilled yet for lock sets. Walking through the house, I'd stop when no one could see me, close my eyes, and sniff the familiar damp-plaster, new-wood fragrance of a just-finished house. Then I'd open my eyes and wonder at the magnificent brand-new old mansion in which, incredibly, I stood.

Sam wanted speed, and got it. When the completed house was still wet with paint, new grass was showing on the landscaped grounds, and transplanted bushes almost surrounded it. He'd had a dozen fir trees trucked to and planted on the grounds at whatever enormous cost—full-grown trees taller than the roof. And five stone masons, all I'd been able to round up, were building a wall clear around the grounds using old gray stone from a dismantled church. And now, the activity of building over and the house painted—entirely white—it lost its visual novelty and took its place in the town. People pausing on the walk dwindled to an occasional one or two.

The day Ellie finished furnishing it she stopped at my office downtown and invited me to see it. We drove in her car, and when we reached the house the great wrought-iron gates stood open in the wall and we swung through them onto a snow-white gravel driveway that curved up to the shaded veranda.

Ellie stopped halfway, giving me a chance to look around. All trace of raw newness was gone; the grounds were lush. This was June and the immense lawns were a flawless, fresh-mowed, brilliant summer green. The hedges were perfectly trimmed and flower beds stood in full bloom.

The house itself was immaculate; it sparkled. It stood there in the splendor of its grounds like a new-cut jewel in a just-finished setting—solid and vigorous, in the very prime of its youth—the living and finished reality of drawings that had lain dustily on my shelves for years.

I had only an impression of the interior when we'd finished—of large-patterned wallpaper suggesting the nineteenth century but colorful, gay, wonderfully cheerful; of last-century furniture intricately but beautifully carved, ornately but gracefully curved, finished to perfection and upholstered in tufted velvets of emerald green, canary yellow, scarlet, coral, and sky blue. I remember a little dressing room carpeted in pink. All doors were dull white, with polished brass hardware. The house sang.

I was out of town on a job the night of the Cluetts' big party a week later, the housewarming. But I drove back late in the evening and, while I wasn't dressed to go inside, I stopped my car by the big iron gates and what I saw was the most haunting sight I've ever seen.

The house was equipped with two lighting systems. One, which I designed, was electric with concealed outlets and almost unnoticeable flush ceiling lights. The other was gas, the lines following the original plans and with ornate fixtures which Ellie had searched out and bought, in all the principal rooms. Tonight as I sat looking in through the big gates, only the gas system was in use. And on all three floors of the big, rambling house, every window—tall and arched at the tops, looking like rows of great slender candles—glowed against the blue summer night with the yellowy, wonderfully warm light electricity has never equaled.

Dancing couples moved across those rectangles of light and music from a live orchestra moved out through the open windows across the lawns into the darkness. Sam had bought a horse and carriage to meet his New York guests at the railroad station. Tonight he'd hired three more and now they all stood on the white gravel of the curved driveway. Any guest who'd come by car had parked in the street. This was one of the last June nights and the air was balmy and alive with the drone of insects, the very sound of summer; and the lawns, strung with candlelit Japanese lanterns, flickered with fireflies. From the veranda I could hear laughter and the murmur of voices softened by distance and people stood outlined on the glowing candle shapes of the windows. Over and enclosing it all, the backdrop for everything, stood the great dark silhouette of the turreted, dormered, many-gabled house. It was a scene lost to the world, a glimpse of another time and manner of living, and I sat there for a long time before I drove home.

You lose touch with clients fairly quickly once a house is finished. For a time you're in each other's company and minds every day, more intimate than friends. Then suddenly you're busy with someone else. I didn't see the Cluetts again till well after Labor Day. Then one afternoon on impulse, I stopped in, not sure if they were still there. But they were. Sam met me on the porch in shirt sleeves—it was warm yet—calling to Ellie that I was there. He led me to the end of the veranda. There was a wooden porch swing, and we sat down, lifting our feet to the porch railing.

I said, "No work today, Sam?"

He smiled. "No. Lately I've been taking more time off than I used to."

From the window behind me, I heard steps in the kitchen, and the sound of glassware. Then Ellie appeared in the doorway.

I stared in open astonishment. Ellie—smiling mischievously as she bent forward to set a tray on a little wicker table—was wearing a dress that began high at the neck and snug around it and ended well below her ankles, brushing the porch floor.

It was a soft leaf green and the long sleeves ended at the wrists in lace cuffs. The upper arms weren't actually puffed but they were full, peaking up a little at the shoulders. It was a dress of the last century and as Ellie sat down I saw that her hair was long now. It was parted in the center and braided and coiled at the back into a flat disk covering the nape of her neck.

Sam was grinning. He said, "You wouldn't want us to be the only things in the house that weren't appropriate, would you, Harry? Ellie and I decided we ought to be dressed for the place." With his fingers he flicked one of his cream-colored pants legs and I saw that they were patterned with a light-blue stripe, a kind of trousers last worn decades ago. Then I realized that his hair wasn't just overdue for cutting; he was wearing it in a style outmoded when my father was born.

I grinned, too, then. Ellie was pouring from a brown stoneware pitcher beaded with tight little drops, the ice clinking as it slid into the glasses. I said, "You look wonderful, both of you; absolutely right for this house. Your guests must get a kick out of it."

"Well, as a matter of fact," Sam said, "we've pretty well quit entertaining my customers here. Not many of them really appreciated the place."

Ellie handed me a filled glass, and I tasted the drink; it was fresh-squeezed lemonade, and delicious. I said, "You must like the house for its own sake, then."

"I can't tell you how much," Ellie said softly. "We've moved here permanently, you know. We don't go to New York any more."

For half an hour, then, we talked about the house. Ellie told me she even sewed here in a little room at the top of a turret. It was something she'd never before had patience for but she'd actually made the dress she was wearing. She said the pattern for it and even the exact shade just came drifting into her mind one day and she wanted to have it and made it herself.

Presently she said, "I always assumed that the plans for this house had never been used, didn't you, Harry?" I nodded, and she said, "But it's just as possible that they *were* used, isn't it?"

"I suppose so."

She smiled wonderingly. "Strange, isn't it, to think that this house existed before? Right here in Darley, undoubtedly, maybe in sight of this one."

"If it existed."

She looked at me for a moment, her face dead serious. Then, with such quiet certainty that I smiled in surprise, she said, "It did."

"Oh? How do you know?"

Ellie looked at Sam. He hesitated, then nodded slightly, and Ellie turned back to me. She said, "You know how associations slowly form in a house you've lived in for a long time. The way the sun strikes the ceiling of a certain room may remind you forever of how it felt when you were a child getting dressed for school. Do you know what I mean?"

I said, "Sure. After a hot day, the beams of my house cool off and contract; make a lot of noise. Every time it happens I remember the first time I tasted strawberries as a kid. With some of the other old associations in my house, the memories are gone, only the emotions left, and I can't remember why they began."

"Yes!" Ellie leaned forward, excited. "This house is full of them! Turn a corner in the front hallway, and the way the stairs rise toward the second floor gives me a feeling of peace. And when the back screen door slams, just the sound of it makes me happy for no reason I know." She hesitated, then said, "And there are other more specific things. One morning

I walked into the library. Sam was sitting there reading. The windowpanes are divided into quarters, and the sun came through at an angle, and four diamond-shaped patches of sunlight lay across the bindings of the books on the shelves. Harry, I saw them, smiled, and said to Sam, 'Well, the Pelliers arrive tomorrow for a week. Won't we have fun!' And Sam looked up and nodded. He knew it, too! Then we just stared at each other. Because we don't know anyone named Pellier; we never have. And no one was coming next day."

Sam said, "I thought she was nuts, too, Harry, till that happened. But from then on, things happened to me, too. There's an upstairs window, and when you open it, it squeals and the sash weight rattles. All I can tell you is that whenever that happens I'm just glad to be alive. And a couple of months ago I opened the front door to see if the morning paper had arrived. My hand touched the doorknob and the instant I felt it—it's porcelain and oval; feels like a china egg—I thought, *Today's the parade!* At the same time, I knew there wasn't any parade, hadn't been a parade in Darley for years." He turned to Ellie. "Tell him about the skating."

She said, "Night before last we were reading in the living room. I looked up from my book at the fireplace, then thought, *In a couple of months, we'll be lighting that. And when we do, there'll be skating on Sikermann's Slough.* Yet I don't even know what that means."

I felt the hair on the back of my neck prickle as I said, "I do. It's been filled in and forgotten for years but it was still there when my father was a boy—a slough that used to freeze over every winter. It was on a corner of what was once the Sikermann farm, sometime in the eighteen eighties."

In Darley, as elsewhere, building slacks off during the winter; and whenever I had time, I tried to learn where or when the old house existed before but I never did. The title block of the original plans tells for whom they were drawn but I found nothing about him or the plans in town records which isn't particularly surprising. I poked through back files of the old Darley *Intelligencer,* too, but found out very little; they're incomplete with gaps of days, weeks, months, and even years. All I learned was how many more fires there were back in the days of largely wood construction and of gas and kerosene lighting and wood stoves.

But I have no doubt that that house existed—sometime in the eighties, I should think. And that it was a happy house—one of the occasional rare and wonderful houses that acquire souls and lives of their own; the kind of house that seems to know you're in it and puts its best foot forward; a house born of the feelings and love of the lost and forgotten people who planned, built, lived in, and gave it life. I think that like many another house of the times this one burned and that maybe my granddad produced the plans for a fire-insurance claim agent, then stuck them on his shelves. I don't know.

But in one way or another its life was cut suddenly short. And then, miraculously, it found itself in being again. Room for room, in every least detail—exactly as it had been in the far-off moment when fire flared along the edge of a curtain, perhaps—the old house existed once more. And it simply resumed its life; the kind of life and times, of course, that it knew.

I've never gone back to it. I suppose I'd be welcome but I don't feel that I belong there any more, not in the life the Cluetts lead now. They leave the grounds only when necessary, Sam driving his buggy. No one goes in; the big gates are kept closed. Sam sold his boatyard this spring—for enough money, I've heard, so that he need never work again. They no longer take a newspaper and whether they read their mail no one knows; they never send any.

But every night the lights are on, the wonderfully warm yellow-orange gas lights, and all last winter they used the fireplaces. This summer people have had glimpses of them. They've been seen playing croquet on the lawn, Ellie in a long white dress. And just this week twin hammocks, the kind with long fringe at the sides, appeared on the shaded veranda. And the two of them lie there reading the lazy afternoons away. I know what they read. The books they'd bought had arrived when I last visited the Cluetts, and along with other fine leather-bound old volumes there were the complete works of Dickens and Sir Walter Scott, just the thing for long summer afternoons far back in the past.

For that's where the Cluetts are, of course. I don't quite believe stories I've heard—that one night last winter it snowed on their property and nowhere else; and that occasionally sun has shone or rain has fallen on their roof but not on the rest of the town, as though the house existed in some other year. Just the same, Ellie and Sam are living far back in the past; that's where they are. For their new house is haunted by its old self. And its ghost has captured the Cluetts—rather easily; I think they were glad to surrender.

The Face in the Photo

On one of the upper floors of the new Hall of Justice I found the room number I was looking for, and opened the door. A nice-looking girl inside glanced up from her typewriter, switched on a smile, and said, "Professor Weygand?" It was a question in form only—one glance at me, and she knew—and I smiled and nodded, wishing I'd worn my have-fun-in-San-Francisco clothes instead of my professor's outfit. She said, "Inspector Ihren's on the phone; would you wait, please?" and I nodded and sat down, smiling benignly the way a professor should.

My trouble is that, although I have the thin, intent, professorial face, I'm a little young for my job, which is assistant professor of physics at a large university. Fortunately I've had some premature gray in my hair ever since I was nineteen, and on campus I generally wear those miserable permanently baggy tweeds that professors are supposed to wear, though a lot of them cheat and don't. These suits, together with round, metal-rimmed, professor-style glasses which I don't really need, and a careful selection of burlap neckties in diseased plaids of bright orange, baboon blue, and gang green (*de rigueur* for gap-pocketed professor suits) complete the image. That's a highly popular word meaning that if you ever want to become a full professor you've got to quit looking like an undergraduate.

I glanced around the little anteroom: yellow plaster walls; a big calendar; filing cabinets; a desk, typewriter, and girl. I watched her the way I inspect some of my more advanced girl students—from under the brows and with a fatherly smile in case she looked up and caught me. What I really wanted to do, though, was pull out Inspector Ihren's letter and read it again for any clue I might have missed about why he wanted to see me. But I'm a little afraid of the police—I get a feeling of guilt just asking a cop a street direction—and I thought rereading the letter just now would betray my nervousness to Miss Candyhips here who would somehow secretly signal the inspector. I knew exactly what it said, anyway. It was a formally polite three-line request, addressed to my office on the campus, to come here and see Inspector Martin O. Ihren, if I would, at my convenience, if I didn't mind, please, sir. I sat wondering what he'd have done if, equally politely, I'd refused, when a buzzer buzzed, the smile turned on again, and the girl said, "Go right in, Professor." I got up, swallowing nervously, opened the door beside me, and walked into the Inspector's office.

Behind his desk he stood up slowly and reluctantly as though he weren't at all sure but what he'd be throwing me into a cell soon. He put out a hand suspiciously and without a smile saying, "Nice of you to come." I answered, sat down before his desk, and I thought I knew what would have happened if I'd refused this man's invitation. He'd simply have arrived in my classroom, clapped on the handcuffs, and dragged me here. I don't mean that his face was forbidding or in any way remarkable; it looked ordinary enough. So did his brown hair and so did his plain gray suit. He was a young-middle-aged man somewhat taller and heavier than I was, and his eyes looked absolutely uninterested in anything in the universe but his work. I had the certain conviction that, except for crime news, he read nothing, not even newspaper headlines; that he was intelligent, shrewd, perceptive, and humorless; and that he probably knew no one but other policemen and didn't think much of most of them. He was an undistinguished formidable man, and I knew my smile looked nervous.

He got right to the point; he was more used to arresting people than dealing with them socially. He said, "There's some people we can't find, and I thought maybe you could help us." I looked politely puzzled but he ignored it. "One of them worked in Haring's Restaurant; you know the place; been there for years. He was a waiter and he disappeared at the end of a three-day weekend with their entire receipts—nearly five thousand bucks. Left a note saying he liked Haring's and enjoyed working there but they'd been underpaying him for ten years and now he figured they were even. Guy with an oddball sense of humor, they tell me." Ihren leaned back in his swivel chair, and frowned at me. "We can't find that man. He's been gone over a year now, and not a trace of him."

I thought he expected me to say something, and did my best. "Maybe he moved to some other city, and changed his name."

Ihren looked startled, as though I'd said something even more stupid than he expected. "That wouldn't help!" he said irritatedly.

I was tired of feeling intimidated. Bravely I said, "Why not?"

"People don't steal in order to hole up forever; they steal money to spend it. His money's gone now, he feels forgotten, and he's got a job again somewhere—as a waiter." I looked skeptical, I suppose, because Ihren said, "Certainly as a waiter; he won't change jobs. That's all he knows, all he can do. Remember John Carradine, the movie actor? Used to see him a lot. Had a face a foot long, all chin and long jaw; very distinctive." I nodded, and Ihren turned in his swivel chair to a filing cabinet. He opened a folder, brought out a glossy sheet of paper, and handed it to me. It was a police WANTED poster, and while the photograph on it did not really resemble the movie actor it had the same remarkable long-jawed memorability. Ihren said, "He could move and he could change his name, but he could never change that face. Wherever he is he should have been found months ago; that poster went everywhere."

I shrugged, and Ihren swung to the file again. He brought out, and handed me, a large old-fashioned sepia photograph mounted on heavy gray cardboard. It was a group photo of a kind you seldom see any more—all the employees of a small business lined up on the sidewalk before it. There were a dozen mustached men in this and a woman in a long dress smiling and squinting in the sun as they stood before a small building which I recognized. It was Haring's Restaurant looking not too different than it does now. Ihren said, "I spotted this on the wall of the restaurant office; I don't suppose anyone has really looked at it in years. The big guy in the middle is the original owner who started the restaurant in 1885 when this was taken; no one knows who anyone else in the picture was but take a good look at the other faces."

I did, and saw what he meant; a face in the old picture almost identical with the one in the WANTED poster. It had the same astonishing length, the broad chin seeming nearly as wide as the cheekbones, and I looked up at Ihren. "Who is it? His father? His grandfather?"

Almost reluctantly he said, "Maybe. It could be, of course. But he sure looks like the guy we're hunting for, doesn't he? And look how he's grinning! Almost as though he'd deliberately gotten a job in Haring's Restaurant again, and were back in 1885 laughing at me!"

I said, "Inspector, you're being extremely interesting, not to say downright entertaining. You've got my full attention, believe me, and I am in no hurry to go anywhere else. But I don't quite see . . ."

"Well, you're a professor, aren't you? And professors are smart, aren't they? I'm looking for help anywhere I can get it. We've got half a dozen unsolved cases like that—people that absolutely should have been found, and found easy! William Spangler Greeson is another one; you ever heard of him?"

"Sure. Who hasn't in San Francisco?"

"That's right, big society name. But did you know he didn't have a dime of his own?"

I shrugged. "How should I know? I'd have assumed he was rich."

"His wife is; I suppose that's why he married her, though they tell me she chased him. She's older than he is, quite a lot. Disagreeable woman; I've talked to her. He's a young, handsome, likable guy, they say, but lazy; so he married her."

"I've seen him mentioned in Herb Caen's column. Had something to do with the theater, didn't he?"

"Stage-struck all his life; tried to be an actor and couldn't make it. When they got married she gave him the money to back a play in New York, which kept him happy for a while; used to fly East a lot for rehearsals and out-of-town tryouts. Then he started getting friendly with some of the younger stage people, the good-looking female ones. His wife punished him like a kid. Hustled him back here, and not a dime for the theater from then on. Money for anything else but he couldn't even buy a ticket to a play any more; he'd been a bad boy. So he disappeared with a hundred and seventy thousand bucks of hers, and not a sign of him since, which just isn't natural. Because he can't—you understand, he *can't*—keep away from the theater. He should have shown up in New York long since—with a fake name, dyed hair, a mustache, some such nonsense. We should have had him months ago but we haven't; he's gone, too." Ihren stood up. "I hope you meant it when you said you weren't in a hurry, because . . ."

"Well, as a matter of fact . . ."

". . . because I made an appointment for both of us. On Powell Street near the Embarcadero. Come on." He walked out from behind his desk, picking up a large Manila envelope lying on one corner of it. There was a New York Police Department return address on the envelope, I saw, and it was addressed to him. He walked to the door without looking back as though he knew I'd follow. Down in front of the building he said, "We can take a cab; with you along I can turn in a chit for it. When I went by myself I rode the cable car."

"On a day like this anyone who takes a cab when he can ride the cable car is crazy enough to join the police force."

Ihren said, "Okay, tourist," and we walked all the way up to Market and Powell in silence. A cable car had just been swung around on its turntable, and we got an outside seat, no one near us; presently the car began crawling and clanging leisurely up Powell. You can sit outdoors on the cable cars, you know, and it was nice out, plenty of sun and blue sky, a typical late summer San Francisco day. But Ihren might as well have been on the New York subway. "So where is William Spangler Greeson?" he said as soon as he'd paid our fares. "Well, on a hunch I wrote the New York police, and they had a man put in a few hours for me at the city historical museum." Ihren opened his Manila envelope, pulled out several folded sheets of grayish paper, and handed the top one to me. I opened it; it was a photostatic copy of an old-style playbill, narrow and long. "Ever hear of that play?" Ihren said, reading over my shoulder. The sheet was headed: TONIGHT & ALL WEEK! SEVEN GALA NIGHTS! Below that, in big type: MABLE'S GREENHORN UNCLE!

"Sure, who hasn't?" I said. "Shakespeare, isn't it?" We were passing Union Square and the St. Francis Hotel.

"Save the jokes for your students, and read the cast of characters."

I read it, a long list of names; there were nearly as many people in old-time plays as in the audiences. At the bottom of the list it said *Members of the Street Crowd,* followed by a dozen or more names in the middle of which appeared William Spangler Greeson.

Ihren said, "That play was given in 1906. Here's another from the winter of 1901." He handed me a second photostat, pointing to another listing at the bottom of the cast. *Onlookers at the Big Race,* this one said, and it was followed by a half-inch of names in small type, the third of which was William Spangler Greeson. "I've got copies of two more playbills," Ihren said, "one from 1902, the other from 1904, each with his name in the cast."

The car swung off Powell, and we hopped off, and continued walking north on Powell. Handing back the photostat, I said, "It's his grandfather. Probably Greeson inherited his interest in the stage from him."

"You're finding a lot of grandfathers today, aren't you, Professor?" Ihren was replacing the stats in their envelopes.

"And what are you finding, Inspector?"

"I'll show you in a minute," he said, and we walked on in silence. We could see the Bay up ahead now, beyond the end of Powell Street, and it looked beautiful in the sun, but Inspector Ihren didn't look at it. We were beside a low concrete building, and he gestured at it with his chin; a sign beside the door read, STUDIO SIXTEEN: COMMERCIAL TV. We walked in, passed through a small office in which no one was present and into an enormous concrete-floored room in which a carpenter was building a set—the front wall of a little cottage. On through that room—the Inspector had obviously been here before—then he pulled open a pair of double doors, and we walked into a tiny movie theater. There was a blank screen up front, a dozen seats, and a projection booth. From the booth a man's voice called, "Inspector?"

"Yeah. You ready?"

"Soon as I thread up."

"Okay." Ihren motioned me to a seat, and sat down beside me. Conversationally he said, "There used to be a minor character around town name of Tom Veeley, a sports fan, a nut. Went to every fight, every Giant and Forty-Niners game, every auto race, roller derby, and jai-alai exhibition that came to town—and complained about them all. We knew him because every once in a while he'd leave his wife. She hated sports, she'd nag him, he'd leave, and we'd have to pick him up on her complaint for desertion and nonsupport; he never got far away. Even when we'd nab him all he'd talk about was how sports were dead, the public didn't care any more and neither did the players, and he wished he'd been around in the really great days of sports. Know what I mean?"

I nodded, the tiny theater went dark, and a beam of sharp white light flashed out over our heads. Then a movie appeared on the screen before us. It was black and white, square in shape, the motion somewhat more rapid and jerky than we're used to, and it was silent. There wasn't even any music, and it was eerie to watch the movement hearing no sound but the whir of the projector. The picture was a view of Yankee Stadium taken from far back of third base showing the stands, a man at bat, the pitcher winding up. Then it switched to a closeup—Babe Ruth at the plate, bat on shoulder, wire backstop in the background, fans behind it. He swung hard, hit the ball, and—chin rising as he followed its flight—he trotted forward. Grinning, his fists pumping rhythmically, he jogged around the bases. Type matter flashed onto the screen: *The Babe does it again!* it began, and went on to say that this was his fifty-first home run of the 1927 season, and that it looked as though Ruth would set a new record.

The screen went blank except for some meaningless scribbled numbers and perforations flying past, and Ihren said, "A Hollywood picture studio arranged this for me, no charge. Sometimes they film cops-and-crooks television up here, so they like to cooperate with us."

Jack Dempsey suddenly appeared on the screen, sitting on a stool in a ring corner, men working over him. It was a poor picture; the ring was outdoors and there was too much sun. But it was Dempsey, all right, maybe twenty-four years old, unshaven and scowling. Around the edge of the ring, the camera panning over them now between rounds, sat men in flat-topped straw hats and stiff collars; some had handkerchiefs tucked into their collars and others were mopping their faces. Then, in the strange silence, Dempsey sprang up and moved out into the ring, crouching very low, and began sparring with an enormous slow-moving opponent; Jess Willard, I imagined. Abruptly the picture ended, the screen illuminated with only a flickering white light. Ihren said, "I looked through nearly six hours of stuff like this; everything from Red Grange to Gertrude Ederle. I pulled out three shots; here's the last one."

On the screen the scratched flickering film showed a golfer sighting for a putt; spectators stood three and four deep around the edge of the green. The golfer smiled engagingly and began waggling his putter; he wore knickers well down below his knees and his hair was parted in the middle and combed straight back. It was Bobby Jones, one of the world's great golfers, at the height of his career back in the 1920s. He tapped the ball, it rolled, dropped into the cup, and Jones hurried after it as the crowd broke onto the green to follow him—all except one man. Grinning, one man walked straight toward the camera, then stopped, doffed his cloth cap in a kind of salute, and bowed from the waist. The camera swung past him to follow Jones who was stooping to retrieve his ball. Then Jones moved on, the man who had bowed to us hurrying after him with the crowd, across the screen and out of sight forever. Abruptly the picture ended, and the ceiling lights came on.

Ihren turned to face me. "That was Veeley," he said, "and it's no use trying to convince me it was his grandfather, so don't try. He wasn't even born when Bobby Jones was winning golf championships, but just the same that was absolutely and indisputably Tom Veeley, the sports fan who's been missing from San Francisco for six months now." He sat waiting, but I didn't reply; what could I say to that? Ihren went on, "He's also sitting just back of home plate behind the screen when Ruth hit the home run, though his face is in shadow. And I think he's one of the men mopping his face at ringside during the Dempsey fight, though I'm not absolutely certain."

The projection-booth door opened, the projectionist came out, saying, "That all today, Inspector?" and Ihren said yeah. The projectionist glanced at me, said, "Hi, Professor," and left.

Ihren nodded. "Yeah, he knows you, Professor. He remembers you. Last week when he ran off this stuff for me, we came to the Bobby Jones film. He remarked that he'd run that on off for someone else only a few days before. I asked who it was, and he said a professor from the university named Weygand. Professor, we must be the only two people in the world interested in that one little strip of film. So I checked on you; you were an assistant professor of physics, brilliant and with a fine reputation, but that didn't help me. You had no criminal record, not with us, anyway, but that didn't tell me anything either; most people have no criminal record, and at least half of them ought to. Then I checked with the newspapers, and the *Chronicle* had a clipping about you filed in their morgue. Come on"—Ihren stood up—"let's get out of here."

Outside, he turned toward the Bay, and we walked to the end of the street, then out onto a wooden pier. A big tanker, her red-painted bottom high out of the water, was sailing past, but Ihren didn't glance at her. He sat down on a piling, motioning me to another beside him, and pulled a newspaper clipping from his breast pocket. "According to this, you gave a talk before the American-Canadian Society of Physicists in June, 1961, at the Fairmont Hotel."

"Is that a crime?"

"Maybe; I didn't hear it. You spoke on 'Some Physical Aspects of Time,' the clipping says. But I don't claim I understood the rest."

"It was a pretty technical talk."

"I got the idea, though, that you thought it might actually be possible to send a man back to an earlier time."

I smiled. "Lots of people have thought so, including Einstein. It's a widely held theory. But that's all, Inspector; just a theory."

"Then let's talk about something that's more than a theory. For over a year San Francisco has been a very good market for old-style currency; I just found that out. Every coin and stamp dealer in town has had new customers, odd ones who didn't give their names and who didn't care what condition the old money was in. The more worn, dirty and creased—and therefore cheaper—the better they liked it, in fact. One of these customers, about a year ago, was a man with a remarkably long thin face. He bought bills and a few coins; any kind at all suited him just as long as they were no later than 1885. Another customer was a young, good-looking, agreeable guy who wanted bills no later than the early 1900s. And so on. Do you know why I brought you out on this dock?"

"No."

He gestured at the long stretch of empty pier behind us. "Because there's no one within a block of us; no witnesses. So tell me, Professor—I can't use what you say, uncorroborated, as evidence—how the hell did you do it? I think you'd like to tell someone; it might as well be me."

Astonishingly, he was right; I *did* want to tell someone, very much. Quickly, before I could change my mind, I said, "I use a little black box with knobs on it, brass knobs." I stopped, stared for a few seconds at a white Coast Guard cutter sliding into view from behind Angel Island, then shrugged and turned back to Ihren. "But you aren't a physicist; how can I explain? All I can tell you is that it really *is* possible to send a man into an earlier time. Far easier, in fact, than any of the theorists had supposed. I adjust the knobs, the dials, focusing the black box on the subject like a camera, as it were. Then"—I shrugged again—"well, I switch on a very faint specialized kind of precisely directed electric current or beam. And while my current is on—how shall I put it? He is afloat, in a manner of speaking; he is actually free of time, which moves on ahead without him. I've calculated that he is adrift, the past catching up with him at a rate of twenty-three years and eleven weeks for each second my current is on. Using a stopwatch, I can send a man back to whatever time he wishes with a plus or minus accuracy of three weeks. I know it works because—well, Tom Veeley is only one example. They all try to do something to show me they arrived safely, and Veeley said he'd do his best to get into the newsreel shot when Jones won the Open Golf Championship. I checked the newsreel last week to make sure he had."

The inspector nodded. "All right; now, *why* did you do it? They're criminals, you know; and you helped them escape."

I said, "No, I didn't know they were criminals, Inspector. And they didn't tell me. They just seemed like nice people with more troubles than they could handle. And I did it because I needed what a doctor needs when he discovers a new serum—volunteers to try it! And I got them; you're not the only one who ever read that news report."

"Where'd you do it?"

"Out on the beach not far from the Cliff House. Late at night when no one was around."

"Why out there?"

"There's some danger a man might appear in a time and place already occupied by something else, a stone wall or building, his molecules occupying the same space. He'd be all mixed in with the other molecules, which would be unpleasant and confining. But there've never been any buildings on the beach. Of course the beach might have been a little higher at one time than another, so I took no chances. I had each of them stand on the lifeguard tower, appropriately dressed for whatever time he planned to enter, and with the right kind of money for the period in his pocket. I'd focus carefully around him so as to exclude the tower, turn on the current for the proper time, and he'd drop onto the beach of fifty, sixty, seventy, or eighty years ago."

For a while the inspector sat nodding, staring absently at the rough planks of the pier. Then he looked up at me again, vigorously rubbing his palms together. "All right, Professor, and now you're going to bring them all back!" I began shaking my head, and he smiled grimly and said, "Oh, yes, you are, or I'll wreck your career! I can do it, you know. I'll bring out everything I've told you, and I'll show the connections. Each of the missing people visited you more than once. Undoubtedly some of them were seen. You may even have been seen on the beach. Time I'm through, you'll never teach again." I was still shaking my head, and he said dangerously, "You mean you won't?"

"I mean I can't, you idiot! How the hell can I reach them? They're back in 1885, 1906, 1927, or whatever; it's absolutely impossible to bring them back. They've escaped you, Inspector—forever."

He actually turned white. "No!" he cried. *"No;* they're criminals and they've got to be punished, *got* to be!"

I was astounded. "Why? None of them's done any great harm. And as far as we're concerned, they don't exist. Forget them."

He actually bared his teeth. "Never," he whispered, then he roared, "I *never* forget a wanted man!"

"Okay, Javert."

"Who?"

"A fictional policeman in a book called *Les Misérables.* He spent half his life hunting down a man no one else wanted any more."

"Good man; like to have him in the department."

"He's not generally regarded too highly."

"He is by me!" Inspector Ihren began slowly pounding his fist into his palm, muttering, "They've got to be punished, they've got to be punished," then he looked up at me. "Get *out* of here," he yelled, *"fast!"* and I was glad to, and did. A block away I looked back, and he was still sitting there on the dock slowly pounding his fist in his palm.

I thought I'd seen the last of him then but I hadn't; I saw Inspector Ihren one more time. Late one evening about ten days later he phoned my apartment and asked me—ordered me—to come right over with my little black box, and I did even though I'd been getting ready for bed; he simply wasn't a man you disobeyed lightly. When I walked up to the big dark Hall of Justice he was standing in the doorway, and without a word he nodded at a car at the curb. We got in, and drove in silence out to a quiet little residential district.

The streets were empty, the houses dark; it was close to midnight. We parked just within range of a corner street light, and Ihren said, "I've been doing some thinking since I saw you last, and some research." He pointed to a mailbox beside the street lamp on the corner a dozen feet ahead. "That's one of the three mailboxes in the city of San Francisco that has been in the same location for almost ninety years. Not that identical box, of course, but always that location. And now we're going to mail some letters." From his coat pocket, Inspector Ihren brought out a little sheaf of envelopes, addressed in pen and ink, and stamped for mailing. He showed me the top one, shoving the others into his pocket. "You see who this is for?"

"The chief of police."

"That's right; the San Francisco chief of police—in 1885! That's his name, address, and the kind of stamp they used then. I'm going to walk to the mailbox on the corner, and hold this in the slot. You'll focus your little black box on the envelope, turn on the current as I let it go, and it will drop into the mailbox that stood here in 1885!"

I shook my head admiringly; it was ingenious. "And what does the letter say?"

He grinned evilly. "I'll tell you what it says! Every spare moment I've had since I last saw you, I've been reading old newspapers at the library. In December, 1884, there was a robbery, several thousand dollars missing; there isn't a word in the paper for months afterward that it was ever solved." He held up the envelope. "Well, this letter suggests to the chief of police that they investigate a man they'll find working in Haring's Restaurant, a man with an unusually long thin face. And that if they search his room, they'll probably find several thousand dollars he can't account for. And that he will absolutely *not* have an alibi for the robbery in 1884!" The Inspector smiled, if you could call it a smile. "That's all they'll need to send him to San Quentin, and mark the case closed; they didn't pamper criminals in those days!"

My jaw was hanging open. "But he isn't guilty! Not of that crime!"

"He's guilty of another just about like it! And he's got to be punished; I *will* not let him escape, not even to 1885!"

"And the other letters?"

"You can guess. There's one for each of the men you helped get away, addressed to the police of the proper time and place. And you're going to help me mail them all, one by one. If you don't I'll ruin you, and that's a promise, Professor." He opened his door, stepped out, and walked to the corner without even glancing back.

I suppose there are those who will say I should have refused to use my little black box no matter what the consequences to me. Well, maybe I should have, but I didn't. The inspector meant what he said and I knew it, and I wasn't going to have the only career I ever had or wanted be ruined. I did the best I could; I begged and pleaded. I got out of the car with my box; the inspector stood waiting at the mailbox. *"Please* don't make me do this," I said. *"Please!* There's no need! You haven't told anyone else about this, have you?"

"Of course not; I'd be laughed off the force."

"Then forget it! Why hound these poor people? They haven't done so much; they haven't really hurt anyone. Be humane! Forgiving! Your ideas are at complete odds with modern conceptions of criminal rehabilitation!"

I stopped for breath, and he said, "You through, Professor? I hope so, because nothing will ever change my mind. Now, go ahead and use that damn box!" Hopelessly I shrugged, and began adjusting the dials.

I am sure that the most baffling case the San Francisco Bureau of Missing Persons ever had will never be solved. Only two people—Inspector Ihren and I—know the answer, and we're not going to tell. For a short time there was a clue someone might have stumbled onto, but I found it. It was in the rare photographs section of the public library; they've got hundreds of old San Francisco pictures, and I went through them all and found this one. Then I stole it; one more crime added to the list I was guilty of hardly mattered.

Every once in a while I get it out, and look at it; it shows a row of uniformed men lined up in formation before a San Francisco police station. In a way it reminds me of an old movie comedy because each of them wears a tall helmet of felt with a broad turn-down brim, and long uniform coats to the knees. Nearly every one of them wears a drooping mustache, and each holds a long nightstick poised at the shoulder as though ready to bring it down on Chester Conklin's head. Keystone Kops they look like at first glance, but study those faces closely and you change your mind about that. Look especially close at the face of the man at the very end of the row, wearing sergeant's stripes. It looks positively and permanently ferocious, glaring out (or so it always seems) directly at me. It is the implacable face of Martin O. Ihren of the San Francisco police force, back where he really belongs, back where I sent him with my little black box, in the year 1893.

I'm Scared

I'm very badly scared, not so much for myself—I'm a gray-haired man of sixty-six, after all—but for you and everyone else who has not yet lived out his life. For I believe that certain dangerous things have recently begun to happen in the world. They are noticed here and there, idly discussed, then dismissed and forgotten. Yet I am convinced that unless these occurrences are recognized for what they are, the world will be plunged into a nightmare. Judge for yourself.

One evening last winter I came home from a chess club to which I belong. I'm a widower; I live alone in a small but comfortable three-room apartment overlooking lower Fifth Avenue. It was still fairly early, and I switched on a lamp beside my leather easy chair, picked up a murder mystery I'd been reading, and turned on the radio; I did not, I'm sorry to say, notice which station it was tuned to.

The tubes warmed, and the music of an accordion—faint at first, then louder—came from the loud-speaker. Since it was good music for reading, I adjusted the volume control and began to read.

Now, I want to be absolutely factual and accurate about

this, and I do not claim that I paid close attention to the radio. But I do know that presently the music stopped, and an audience applauded. Then a man's voice, chuckling and pleased with the applause, said, "All right, all right," but the applause continued for several more seconds. During that time the voice once more chuckled appreciatively, then firmly repeated, "All right," and the applause died down. "That was Alec Somebody-or-other," the radio voice said, and I went back to my book.

But I soon became aware of this middle-aged voice again; perhaps a change of tone as he turned to a new subject caught my attention. "And now, Miss Ruth Greeley," he was saying, "of Trenton, New Jersey. Miss Greeley is a pianist; that right?" A girl's voice, timid and barely audible, said, "That's right, Major Bowes." The man's voice—and now I recognized his familiar singsong delivery—said, "And what are you going to play?" The girl replied, "La Paloma." The man repeated it after her, as an announcement: "La Paloma." There was a pause, then an introductory chord sounded from a piano, and I resumed my reading.

As the girl played, I was half aware that her style was mechanical, her rhythm defective; perhaps she was nervous. Then my attention was fully aroused once more by a gong which sounded suddenly. For a few notes more the girl continued to play falteringly, not sure what to do. The gong sounded jarringly again, the playing abruptly stopped, and there was a restless murmur from the audience. "All right, all right," said the now familiar voice, and I realized I'd been expecting this, knowing it would say just that. The audience quieted, and the voice began, "Now——"

The radio went dead. For the smallest fraction of a second no sound issued from it but its own mechanical hum. Then a completely different program came from the loudspeaker; the recorded voice of Andy Williams singing, "You Butterfly," a favorite of mine. So I returned once more to my reading, wondering vaguely what had happened to the other program, but not actually thinking about it until I finished my book and began to get ready for bed.

Then, undressing in my bedroom, I remembered that Major Bowes was dead. Years had passed, a decade, since that dry chuckle and familiar, "All right, all right," had been heard in the nation's living rooms.

Well, what does one do when the apparently impossible occurs? It simply made a good story to tell friends, and more than once I was asked if I'd recently heard Moran and Mack, a pair of radio comedians popular some thirty years ago, or Floyd Gibbons, an old-time news broadcaster. And there were other joking references to my crystal radio set.

But one man—this was at a lodge meeting the following Thursday—listened to my story with utter seriousness, and when I had finished he told me a queer little story of his own. He is a thoughtful, intelligent man, and as I listened I was not frightened, but puzzled at what seemed to be a connecting link, a common denominator, between this story and the odd behavior of my radio. The following day, since I am retired and have plenty of time, I took the trouble of making a two-hour train trip to Connecticut in order to verify the story at firsthand. I took detailed notes, and the story appears in my files now as follows:

Case 2. Louis Trachnor, coal and wood dealer, R.F.D. 1, Danbury, Connecticut, aged fifty-four.

On July 20, 1956, Mr. Trachnor told me, he walked out on the front porch of his house about six o'clock in the morning. Running from the eaves of his house to the floor of the porch was a streak of gray paint, still damp. "It was about the width of an eight-inch brush," Mr. Trachnor told me, "and it looked like hell, because the house was white. I figured some kids did it in the night for a joke, but if they did, they had to get a ladder up to the eaves and you wouldn't figure they'd go to that much trouble. It wasn't smeared, either; it was a careful job, a nice even stripe straight down the front of the house."

Mr. Trachnor got a ladder and cleaned off the gray paint with turpentine.

In October of that same year, Mr. Trachnor painted his house. "The white hadn't held up so good, so I painted it gray. I got to the front last and finished about five one Saturday afternoon. Next morning when I came out, I saw a streak of white right down the front of the house. I figured it was the damned kids again, because it was the same place as before. But when I looked close, I saw it wasn't new paint; it was the old white I'd painted over. Somebody had done a nice careful job of cleaning off the new paint in a long stripe about eight inches wide right down from the eaves! Now, who the hell would go to that trouble? I just can't figure it out."

Do you see the link between this story and mine? Suppose for a moment that something had happened, on each occasion, to disturb briefly the orderly progress of time. That seemed to have happened in my case; for a matter of some seconds I apparently heard a radio broadcast that had been made years before. Suppose, then, that no one had touched Mr. Trachnor's house but himself; that he had painted his house in October, and that through some fantastic mix-up in time, a portion of that paint appeared on his house the previous summer. Since he had cleaned the paint off at that time, a broad stripe of new gray paint was missing *after* he painted his house in the fall.

I would be lying, however, if I said I really believed this. It was merely an intriguing speculation, and I told both these little stories to friends, simply as curious anecdotes. I am a sociable person, see a good many people, and occasionally I heard other odd stories in response to mine.

Someone would nod and say, "Reminds me of something I heard recently . . ." and I would have one more to add to my collection. A man on Long Island received a telephone call from his sister in New York on Friday evening. She insists that she did not make this call until the following Monday, three days later. At the Forty-fifth Street branch of the Chase National Bank, I was shown a check deposited the day before it was written. A letter was delivered on East Sixty-eighth Street in New York City, just seventeen minutes after it was dropped into a mailbox on the main street of Green River, Wyoming.

And so on, and so on; my stories were now in demand at parties and I told myself that collecting and verifying them was a hobby. But the day I heard Julia Eisenberg's story, I knew it was no longer that.

Case 17. Julia Eisenberg, office worker, New York City, aged thirty-one.

Miss Eisenberg lives in a small walk-up apartment in Greenwich Village. I talked to her there after a chess-club friend who lives in her neighborhood had repeated to me a somewhat garbled version of her story, which was told to him by the doorman of the building he lives in.

In October, 1954, about eleven at night, Miss Eisenberg left her apartment to walk to the drugstore for toothpaste. On her way back, not far from her apartment, a large black and white dog ran up to her and put his front paws on her chest.

"I made the mistake of petting him," Miss Eisenberg told me, "and from then on he simply wouldn't leave. When I went into the lobby of my building, I actually had to push him away to get the door closed. I felt sorry for him, poor hound, and a little guilty, because he was still sitting at the door an hour later when I looked out my front window."

This dog remained in the neighborhood for three days, discovering and greeting Miss Eisenberg with wild affection each time she appeared on the street. "When I'd get on the bus in the morning to go to work, he'd sit on the curb looking after me in the most mournful way, poor thing. I wanted to take him in, and I wish with all my heart that I had, but I knew he'd never go home then, and I was afraid whoever owned him would be sorry to lose him. No one in the neighborhood knew who he belonged to, and finally he disappeared."

Two years later a friend gave Miss Eisenberg a three-week-old puppy. "My apartment is really too small for a dog, but he was such a darling I couldn't resist. Well, he grew up into a nice big dog who ate more than I did."

Since the neighborhood was quiet, and the dog well behaved, Miss Eisenberg usually unleashed him when she walked him at night, for he never strayed far. "One night—I'd last seen him sniffing around in the dark a few doors down—I called to him and he didn't come back. And he never did; I never saw him again.

"Now, our street is a solid wall of brownstone buildings on both sides, with locked doors and no areaways. He *couldn't* have disappeared like that, he just *couldn't*. But he did."

Miss Eisenberg hunted for her dog for many days afterward, inquired of neighbors, put ads in the papers, but she never found him. "Then one night I was getting ready for bed; I happened to glance out the front window down at the street, and suddenly I remembered something I'd forgotten all about. I remembered the dog I'd chased away over two years before." Miss Eisenberg looked at me for a moment, then she said flatly. "It was the same dog. If you own a dog you *know* him, you can't be mistaken, and I tell you it was the same dog. Whether it makes sense or not, my dog was lost—I chased him away—two years before he was born."

She began to cry silently, the tears running down her face. "Maybe you think I'm crazy, or a little lonely and overly sentimental about a dog. But you're wrong." She brushed at her tears with a handkerchief. "I'm a well-balanced person, as much as anyone is these days, at least, and I tell you I *know* what happened."

It was in that moment, sitting in Miss Eisenberg's neat, shabby living room, that I realized fully that the consequences of these odd little incidents could be something more than merely intriguing; that they might, quite possibly, be tragic. It was in that moment that I began to be afraid.

I have spent the last eleven months discovering and tracking down these strange occurrences, and I am astonished and frightened at how many there are. I am astonished and frightened at how much more frequently they are happening now, and—I hardly know how to express this—at their increasing *power* to tear human lives tragically apart. This is an example, selected almost at random, of the increasing strength of—whatever it is that is happening in the world.

Case 34. Paul V. Kerch, accountant, the Bronx, aged thirty-one.

On a bright, clear, Sunday afternoon, I met an unsmiling family of three at their Bronx apartment: Mr. Kerch, a chunky, darkly good-looking young man; his wife, a pleasant-faced dark-haired woman in her late twenties, whose attractiveness was marred by circles under her eyes; and their son, a nice-looking boy of six or seven. After introductions, the boy was sent to his room at the back of the house to play.

"All right," Mr. Kerch said wearily then, and walked toward a bookcase, "let's get at it. You said on the phone that you know the story in general." It was half a question, half a statement.

"Yes," I said.

He took a book from the top shelf and removed some photographs from it. "There are the pictures." He sat down on the davenport beside me, with the photographs in his hand. "I own a pretty good camera, I'm a fair amateur photographer, and I have a darkroom setup in the kitchen; do my own developing. Two weeks ago, we went down to Central Park." His voice was a tired monotone as though this were a story he'd repeated many times, aloud and in his own mind. "It was nice, like today, and the kid's grandmothers have been pestering us for pictures, so I took a whole roll of films, pictures of all of us. My camera can be set up and focused and it will snap the picture automatically a few seconds later, giving me time to get around in front of it and get in the picture myself."

There was a tired, hopeless look in his eyes as he handed me all but one of the photographs. "These are the first ones I took," he said. The photographs were all fairly large, perhaps 5 × 7″, and I examined them closely.

They were ordinary enough, very sharp and detailed, and each showed the family of three in various smiling poses. Mr. Kerch wore a light business suit, his wife had on a dark dress and a cloth coat, and the boy wore a dark suit with knee-length pants. In the background stood a tree with bare branches. I glanced up at Mr. Kerch, signifying that I had finished my study of the photographs.

"The last picture," he said, holding it in his hand ready to give to me, "I took exactly like the others. We agreed on the pose, I set the camera, walked around in front, and joined my family. Monday night I developed the whole roll. This is what came out on the last negative." He handed me the photograph.

For an instant it seemed to me like merely one more photograph in the group; then I saw the diffrence. Mr. Kerch looked much the same, bare-headed and grinning broadly, but he wore an entirely different suit. The boy, standing beside him, wore long pants, was a good three inches taller, obviously older, but equally obviously the same boy. The woman was an entirely different person. Dressed smartly, her light hair catching the sun, she was very pretty and attractive, and she was smiling into the camera, holding Mr. Kerch's hand.

I looked up at him. "Who is this?"

Wearily, Mr. Kerch shook his head. "I don't know," he said sullenly, then suddenly exploded: "I don't *know!* I've never seen her in my life!" He turned to look at his wife, but she would not return his glance, and he turned back to me, shrugging. "Well, there you have it," he said. "The whole story." And he stood up, thrusting both hands into his trouser pockets, and began to pace about the room, glancing often at his wife, talking to *her* actually, though he addressed his words to me. "So who is she? How could the camera have snapped that picture? I've never seen that woman in my life!"

I glanced at the photograph again, then bent closer. "The trees here are in full bloom," I said. Behind the solemn-faced boy, the grinning man and smiling woman, the trees of Central Park were in full summer leaf.

Mr. Kerch nodded. "I know," he said bitterly. "And you know what *she* says?" he burst out, glaring at his wife. "She says that *is* my wife in the photograph, my *new* wife a couple of years from now! God!" He slapped both hands down on his head. "The ideas a woman can get!"

"What do you mean?" I glanced at Mrs. Kerch, but she ignored me, remaining silent, her lips tight.

Kerch shrugged hopelessly. "She says that photograph shows how things will be a couple of years from now. She'll be dead or"—he hesitated, then said the word bitterly—"divorced, and I'll have our son and be married to the woman in the picture."

We both looked at Mrs. Kerch, waiting until she was obliged to speak.

"Well, if it isn't so," she said, shrugging a shoulder, "then tell me what that picture does mean."

Neither of us could answer that, and a few minutes later I left. There was nothing much I could say to the Kerches; certainly I couldn't mention my conviction that, whatever the explanation of the last photograph, their married life was over. . . .

Case 72. Lieutenant Alfred Eichler, New York Police Department, aged thirty-three.

In the late evening of January 9, 1956, two policemen found a revolver lying just off a gravel path near an East Side entrance to Central Park. The gun was examined for fingerprints at the police laboratory and several were found. One bullet had been fired from the revolver and the police fired another which was studied and classified by a ballistics expert. The fingerprints were checked and found in police files; they were those of a minor hoodlum with a record of assault.

A routine order to pick him up was sent out. A detective called at the rooming house where he was known to live, but he was out, and since no unsolved shootings had occurred recently, no intensive search for him was made that night.

The following evening a man was shot and killed in Central Park with the same gun. This was proved ballistically past all question of error. It was soon learned that the murdered man had been quarreling with a friend in a nearby tavern. The two men, both drunk, had left the tavern together. And the second man was the hoodlum whose gun had been found the previous night, and which was still locked in a police safe.

As Lieutenant Eichler said to me, "It's impossible that the dead man was killed with that same gun, but he was. Don't ask me how, though, and if anybody thinks we'd go into court with a case like that, they're crazy."

Case 111. Captain Hubert V. Rihm, New York Police Department, retired, aged sixty-six.

I met Captain Rihm by appointment one morning in Stuyvesant Park, a patch of greenery, wood benches and asphalt surrounded by the city, on lower Second Avenue. "You want to hear about the Fentz case, do you?" he said, after we had introduced ourselves and found an empty bench. "All right, I'll tell you. I don't like to talk about it—it bothers me—but I'd like to see what you think." He was a big, rather heavy man, with a red, tough face, and he wore an old police jacket and uniform cap with the insigne removed.

"I was up at City Mortuary," he began, as I took out my notebook and pencil, "at Bellevue, about twelve one night, drinking coffee with one of the interns. This was in June, 1955, just before I retired, and I was in Missing Persons. They brought this guy in and he was a funny-looking character. Had a beard. A young guy, maybe thirty, but he wore regular muttonchop whiskers, and his clothes were funny-looking. Now, I was thirty years on the force and I've seen a lot of queer guys killed on the streets. We found an Arab once, in full regalia, and it took us a week to find out who he was. So it wasn't just the way the guy looked that bothered me; it was the stuff we found in his pockets."

Captain Rihm turned on the bench to see if he'd caught my interest, then countinued. "There was about a dollar in change in the dead guy's pocket, and one of the boys picked up a nickel and showed it to me. Now, you've seen plenty of nickels, the news ones with Jefferson's picture, the buffalo nickels they made before that, and once in a while you still see even the old Liberty-head nickels; they quit making them before the First World War. But this one was even older than that. It had a shield on the front, a U.S. shield, and a big five on the back; I used to see that kind when I was a boy. And the funny thing was, that old nickel looked new; what coin dealers call 'mint condition,' like it was made the day before yesterday. The date on that nickel was 1876, and there wasn't a coin in his pocket dated any later."

Captain Rihm looked at me questioningly. "Well," I said, glancing up from my notebook, "that could happen."

"Sure, it could," he answered in a satisfied tone, "but all the pennies he had were Indian-head pennies. Now, when did you see one of them last? There was even a silver three-cent piece; looked like an old-style dime, only smaller. And the bills in his wallet, every one of them, were old-time bills, the big kind."

Captain Rihm leaned forward and spat on the path, a needle-jet of tobacco juice, and an expression of a policeman's annoyed contempt for anything deviating from an orderly norm.

"Over seventy bucks in cash, and not a Federal reserve note in the lot. There were two yellow-back tens. Remember them? They were payable in gold. The rest were old national-bank notes; you remember them, too. Issued direct by local banks, personally signed by the bank president; that kind used to be counterfeited a lot.

"Well," Captain Rihm continued, leaning back on the bench and crossing his knees, "there was a bill in his pocket from a livery stable on Lexington Avenue: three dollars for feeding and stabling his horse and washing a carriage. There was a brass slug in his pocket good for a five-cent beer at some saloon. There was a letter postmarked Philadelphia, June, 1876, with an old-style two-cent stamp; and a bunch of cards in his wallet. The cards had his name and address on them, and so did the letter."

"Oh," I said, a little surprised, "you identified him right away, then?"

"Sure. Rudolph Fentz, some address on Fifth Avenue—I forget the exact number—in New York City. No problem at all." Captain Rihm leaned forward and spat again. "Only that address wasn't a residence. It's a store, and it has been for years, and nobody there ever heard of any Rudolph Fentz, and there's no such name in the phone book, either. Nobody ever called or made any inquiries about the guy, and Washington didn't have his prints. There was a tailor's name in his coat, a lower Broadway address, but nobody there ever heard of this tailor."

"What was so strange about his clothes?"

The Captain said, "Well, did you ever know anyone who wore a pair of pants with big black-and-white checks, cut very narrow, no cuffs, and pressed without a crease?"

I had to think for a moment. "Yes," I said then, "my father, when he was a very young man, before he was married; I've seen old photographs."

"Sure," said Captain Rihm, "and he probably wore a short sort of cutaway coat with two cloth-covered buttons at the back, a vest with lapels, a tall silk hat, and a big, black oversize bow tie on a turned-up stiff collar, and button shoes."

"That's how this man was dressed?"

"Like eighty years ago! And him no more than thirty years old. There was a label in his hat, a Twenty-third Street hat store that went out of business around the turn of the century. Now, what do you make out of a thing like that?"

"Well," I said carefully, "there's nothing much you can make of it. Apparently someone went to a lot of trouble to dress up in an antique style; the coins and bills, I assume he could buy at a coin dealer's; and then he got himself killed in a traffic accident."

"Got himself killed is right. Eleven fifteen at night in Times Square—the theaters letting out; busiest time and place in the world—and this guy shows up in the middle of the street, gawking and looking around at the cars and up at the signs like he'd never seen them before. The cop on duty noticed him, so you can see how he must have been acting. The lights change, the traffic starts up, with him in the middle of the street, and instead of waiting, the damned fool, he turns and tries to make it back to the sidewalk. A cab got him and he was dead when he hit."

For a moment Captain Rihm sat chewing his tobacco and staring angrily at a young woman pushing a baby carriage, though I'm sure he didn't see her. The young mother looked at him in surprise as she passed, and the captain continued:

"Nothing you can make out of a thing like that. We found out nothing. I started checking through our file of old phone books, just as routine, but without much hope because they only go back so far. But in the 1939 summer edition I found a Rudolph Fentz, Jr., somewhere on East Fifty-second Street. He'd moved away in 'forty-two, though, the building super told me, and was a man in his sixties besides, retired from business; used to work in a bank a few blocks away, the super thought. I found the bank where he'd worked, and they told me he'd retired in 'forty, and had been dead for five years; his widow was living in Florida with a sister.

"I wrote to the widow, but there was only one thing she could tell us, and that was no good. I never even reported it, not officially, anyway. Her husband's father had disappeared when her husband was a boy maybe two years old. He went out for a walk around ten one night—his wife thought cigar smoke smelled up the curtains, so he used to take a little stroll before he went to bed, and smoke a cigar—and he didn't come back, and was never seen or heard of again. The family spent a good deal of money trying to locate him, but they never did. This was in the middle eighteen seventies sometime; the old lady wasn't sure of the exact date. Her husband hadn't ever said too much about it.

"And that's all," said Captain Rihm. "Once I put in one of my afternoons off hunting through a bunch of old police records. And I finally found the Missing Persons file for 1876, and Rudolph Fentz was listed, all right. There wasn't much of a description, and no fingerprints, of course. I'd give a year of my life, even now, and maybe sleep better nights, if they'd had his fingerprints. He was listed as twenty-nine years old, wearing full muttonchop whiskers, a tall silk hat, dark coat and checked pants. That's about all it said. Didn't say what kind of tie or vest or if his shoes were the button kind. His name was Rudolph Fentz and he lived at this address on Fifth Avenue; it must have been a residence then. Final disposition of case: not located.

"Now, I hate that case," Captain Rihm said quietly. "I hate it and I wish I'd never heard of it. What do *you* think?" He demanded suddenly, angrily. "You think this guy walked off into thin air in eighteen seventy-six, and showed up again in nineteen fifty-five!"

I shrugged noncommittally, and the captain took it to mean no.

"No, of course not," he said. "Of *course* not, but—give me some other explanation."

I could go on. I could give you several hundred such cases. A sixteen-year-old girl walked out of her bedroom one morning, carrying her clothes in her hand because they were too big for her, and she was quite obviously eleven years old again. And there are other occurrences too horrible for print. All of them have happened in the New York City area alone, all within the last few years; and I suspect thousands more have occurred, and are occurring, all over the world. I could go on, but the point is this: What is happening and *why*? I believe that I know.

Haven't you noticed, too, on the part of nearly everyone you know, a growing rebellion against the *present?* And an increasing longing for the past? I have. Never before in all my long life have I heard so many people wish that they lived "at the turn of the century," or "when life was simpler," or "worth living," or "when you could bring children into the world and count on the future," or simply "in the good old days." People didn't talk that way when I was young! The present was a glorious time! But they talk that way now.

For the first time in man's history, man is desperate to escape the present. Our newsstands are jammed with escape literature, the very name of which is significant. Entire magazines are devoted to fantastic stories of escape—to other times, past and future, to other worlds and planets—escape to anywhere but here and now. Even our larger magazines, book publishers and Hollywood are beginning to meet the rising demand for this kind of escape. Yes, there is a craving in the world like a thirst, a terrible mass pressure that you can almost feel, of millions of minds struggling against the barriers of time. I am utterly convinced that this terrible mass pressure of millions of minds is already, slightly but definitely, affecting time itself. In the moments when this happens—when the almost universal longing to escape is greatest—my incidents occur. Man is disturbing the clock of time, and I am afraid it will break. When it does, I leave to your imagination the last few hours of madness that will be left to us; all the countless moments that now make up our lives suddenly ripped apart and chaotically tangled in time.

Well, I have lived most of my life; I can be robbed of only a few more years. But it seems too bad—this universal craving to escape what could be a rich, productive, happy world. We live on a planet well able to provide a decent life for every soul on it, which is all ninety-nine of a hundred human beings ask. Why in the world can't we have it?

Home Alone

On the sixth day that he was home alone Charley Burke walked out onto the patio, nodded at the empty chairs, saying, "Hello, everybody. Don't get up," and dropped into a lounge chair. He was wearing the tan wash pants and brown loafers he'd just changed into and the white shirt he'd worn that day in San Francisco at the office. Now he tilted far back in the chair, his feet rising higher than his head. It was August, still daylight, and he lay staring up at the clear blue sky. He was conscious of the emptiness of the suburban house beside him but absently so, used to it now. Then his jaw dropped, his eyes widened, and he lay motionless, staring up at the sky, paralyzed by the strength of a strange new emotion.

His house, across the Bay from the city, in Marin County, lay in a miniature valley; the street wound between two rows of hills. Fifty yards above the hills that rose behind the patio a hawk hung in the air high in the sun. He was there often hunting field rodents; Charley had seen him before. But now he saw him, actually, for the first time. The big bird didn't move. Wings out he lay on an invisible column of air that pressed against the sides of the hills to be deflected upward.

He lay there magically neither rising nor falling, moving neither forward nor back, no least movement of his wings necessary to sustain him. Then the wings tilted, the bird dropped in a sudden swift and graceful arc and soared up again. The wings tilted back once more and again the hawk hung in the summer sky belonging to it; and all that Charley Burke wanted of the entire world was somehow to be able to do that, too.

It was no idle wish. It was an overpowering seizure, a wild and passionate necessity. Its intensity drew him to his feet and he walked the patio, smiling, trying to laugh the feeling away. But there was no escape. He was possessed by an irresistible urge to rise in effortless detachment from gravity up into the blueness till he could feel the sky around him touching his skin. And it occurred to him that he could do what he wanted to do—not in a plane fighting the air but in a balloon.

Stepping between the open glass doors, he stood in the living room, neat in the gathering darkness—ashtrays emptied, magazines stacked. But when he snapped on a light the room looked dusty. He stood thinking over all he knew about balloons. Mostly this was just a picture in his mind of a large, rounded object shaped like a giant punching bag upside down in the sky. It was made in vertical panels of contrasting colors, a long ribben pennant fluttered from its top, and under it hung a trapezelike bar on which sat a man wearing tights. He wore his hair parted in the center, had a large mustache, and sat smiling, ankles crossed, legs dangling gracefully, a hand negligently holding to one rope of his perch. Stitched to the chest of his tights was an American flag. This picture was supplanted by another very much like it except that now a square basket with high sides hung under the balloon. A man stood in the basket staring out at him; he wore a black silk hat, black frock coat, square-cut beard, pince-nez, and had a brass telescope tucked under one arm.

That was all Charley knew about balloons. He took down volume two of the encyclopedia on the living-room bookshelves, found the article on balloons, and sat down at one end of the davenport, leaning over the pages. "Balloon," the article began, "a bag of impermeable material which, when inflated with a gas lighter than air, rises from the ground." This had almost the lilt of poetry, he felt, the last four words especially, and he read it through several times, glancing up each time to smile.

Then he read everything in the article about how and why a balloon rises, descends, and is controlled, and it seemed to him as simple and effective a device as man has yet invented. Filled with a gas lighter than the volume of air it displaces, a balloon must rise. Release some of the gas and its ascent is checked or reversed. Spill ballast and its rise will resume. The open book on his lap, Charley sat back, hands clasped behind his head, at peace with this explanation.

It was easily understood without special training, like most of the mechanical devices of the previous century. Men understood the things they used then; they were masters of the machines that served them. He felt sure that passengers riding in hydraulic elevators of the time knew how they worked, and that most men, a forefinger on a sharp-etched woodcut diagram, could trace through the workings of a horsecar mechanism. Of the thousands of years men have been civilized, it is only in the last fifty, Charley thought, that things we use daily have gone beyond the understanding of most of us—our television sets, jet planes, even our automobiles today. Most of us use them in helplessness, no longer their masters, no longer masters of very much at all any more. So that to understand the balloon was a solid satisfaction and Charley stood up and began to sing. It was an ancient song he hadn't thought of in years and the house being empty he shouted it full voice. "Come, Josephine, in my flying machine, and it's *up* we'll go, *up* we'll go!" he yelled in sudden exuberance, and walked quickly to the garage where he began hunting for things he needed, such as his wife's plastic clothesline and two old tennis nets.

Through that and the following two evenings, working hard and steadily, Charley made a balloon. He cut the panels from two rolls of lightweight rubberized cloth—one was blue, and one was white—which he bought in San Francisco, and stitched them together on his wife's sewing machine. With odds and ends around the house—a wire coat hanger, an aluminum pot lid, his wife's clothes pole—he completed the balloon, then hung it from a rope over the patio.

It could turn chilly after the sun was down here in the San Francisco Bay area, and Charley changed into black ski pants and jersey, light in weight but snug-fitting and very warm. Looking down at himself it occurred to him that they somewhat resembled a balloonist's tights, and he smiled. Finally, well after eleven at night, Charley stood on the patio beside the brick barbecue tending a bed of coals. The electric blower was on full, the coals white hot and flameless in the forced draft, and a steady rush of hot air roared up through a stovepipe resting on the grill and into the balloon hanging overhead.

Almost instantly the long blue-and-white wrinkles of hanging cloth rising up into the night over Charley's head had begun to stir; now they were visibly distending. From a long, wrinkled prune the balloon swelled into a thin pear, then rounded into a smooth-skinned sphere. At eleven forty-five the bag, round and tight, began to lift. Within minutes, it seemed alive. Tugging at the anchor rope tied to the barbecue, it swayed in the air fat, buoyant, and eager. Two tennis nets hung draped over it. Tied to their ends by short lengths of clothesline hung a trapezelike seat made from half a clothes pole. Several dozen paper bags imprinted Mill Valley Market and filled with sand hung in the netting.

Charley switched off the barbecue blower and sat on the trapeze. Like a child slowly untying a gift to prolong the anticipation, he began pulling the drawstring that would release his balloon from the anchor rope. At that moment the moon, which had been rising for some minutes, lifted an edge over the uneven horizon of hills. Hanging under the balloon in his black ski suit and a pair of heavy navy-blue wool socks, Charley saw the pale wash of light touch the windows of the empty house beside him and turn them opaque, dimly reflecting himself and the bottom of the balloon like a faded poster from a forgotten circus. Looking up, he watched the moonlight slide up and down the striped sides of the balloon as it swayed and he felt a surge of pride stronger than any he'd felt in years. Of all the things he owned, it suddenly occurred to him, this was the only one he'd created, the only thing he hadn't bought. Of all his possessions this was uniquely his own and, while he knew that what he was about to do could be dangerous, he didn't believe in the danger. His heart beat from joy, not fear, as he yanked hard at the rope in his hand.

Instantly the wooden bar on which he sat pressed deep into the undersides of Charley's legs and he was looking down onto his moonlit roof. Immediately the roofs of his neighbors came sliding into view from the sides; then he was looking at the street in front of his house. It was growing in length, shrinking in width, winding through the hills between two rows of rooftops which were diminishing as he stared into smaller and smaller rectangles and squares.

Up through the moonlight he rose into the night in glorious silence. His only motive power was air itself, air being lifted by air. He was a weightless part of the element he was in mingling with its breezes. Now he rose above the level of the low Marin County hills and here occasional puffs of air touched him and he drifted a little like a ball of dandelion fluff over the light-speckled patches and great dark areas of town and countryside spreading below him. A hand tightly gripping each support rope, Charley sat on his wife's clothes pole swinging slightly, pleasantly, and felt the gentle lift of the bar under his legs slacken and then stop. Mouth agape, eyes wide and heart pounding, he hung in the air staring down between his dangling feet at the tiny roofs and narrow moonlit black ribbon that was the street he lived on.

A breeze touched the balloon momentarily and it slowly revolved. As he turned in the air Charley suddenly saw over his shoulder the great shiny-black expanse of San Francisco Bay far ahead and far below. From ground level it lay behind rows of hills and could not be seen. But hanging up here in the sky he saw it all, saw the mysterious lights of its great bridges—dotted lines of luminous orange-juice-color lights curving across the shiny blackness. A path of moonlight silvered the water between the bridges silhouetting Angel Island, humping up out of the bay, lusterless, black, and lightless. White mast lights and green side lights, the ship itself invisible, moved across the ink-shiny blackness and beyond all this, rising up in light and splendor, was the glorious glitter of San Francisco. The shining city crisscrossed by the pattern of its streets and the vast black Bay edged in light on the Oakland rim were a great living map far below his hanging feet. It was an awesome sight, incredible and beautiful, and Charley shouted in delight.

The slow revolution of the balloon continued and when Charley again faced south the Bay had disappeared, the tops of the hills that concealed it rising beyond his head. The heated air in the balloon cooling in the night, the balloon was sinking and within minutes, he knew, it would gently collapse in the street directly below him. He tried to make it stop by an effort of will, tried to make himself lighter on the bar he sat on. But like an ancient slow-moving elevator, it descended steadily until, well below the level of the surrounding hills, a breeze suddenly took it.

Nearly every night during the summer, beginning just after sunset, an easterly breeze flowed down this street, channeled between the hills like a river. Charley moved with it now, along the curving street toward home, perhaps ten feet above the street lamps moving past him on either side of the road. Down here between the bases of the hills, the breeze narrowed and quickened, and now he moved swiftly, the trapped current carrying him silently along the wide street precisely over the white-painted center line following its curves and winding exactly.

Slipping through the night just over the roofs of the familiar houses, he glanced from one side to the other as he passed. He knew or at least spoke to the people in most of these houses. But now the houses were dark, the cars parked before them dead and silent, their windows blind with dew, and Charley thought of his own empty house and felt suddenly depressed. A cat darted across the street through a circle of light from a street lamp; it stopped suddenly, crouching motionless in the gutter to stare up at him over a shoulder as he swung past.

Just ahead the road curved, and now the breeze curved with

it and Charley swung around the bend nearing his house. His dangling legs swinging from the turn, Charley rounded the curve and a movement ahead caught his eye. Then he saw the big Dalmatian dog trotting briskly beside the curb and just entering a circle of lamplight. This side of the circle he caught the slower movement of a woman in a tan polo coat. He knew who she was. Once or twice, driving home late at night, he had seen her walking this dog. She was a Mrs. Lanidas who lived a dozen houses down the street from his.

There was nothing he could do, there was no time to spill ballast. His feet and half his body were below the level of the glass-shaded street lamp now and his shadow flashed across the circle of light on the lonely asphalt road as Mrs. Lanidas walked into it. She stopped, her chin lifting quickly, and for the space of a heartbeat she and Charley, looking back over his shoulder, stared into each other's eyes. Then Charley swung on around a final bend. Just before his driveway, the balloon sinking fast, his stockinged feet touched the road and he ran, tugging at the tennis nets to bring down the collapsing balloon.

Still running, he swung into his driveway dragging the balloon through the air on the very last of its buoyancy. Then it melted onto the concrete before the garage door in a rustling mass of striped cloth. Stooping quickly, his hand on the door handle, Charley paused for an instant, listening. In the almost complete silence of the late-at-night street he heard the slight grate of leather on pebbles. The steps were hurrying, he thought, and he heaved the garage door up. Tugging, yanking, he dragged the balloon in alongside the car, then grabbed for the garage door. But even as it slid down again, the footsteps stopped and he knew the woman was standing in the street at the end of his driveway staring at the door as it closed.

But nothing could have kept him from going up again. He

got through the next day at the office. At home, even before he changed clothes, he was prowling through the garage, the attic of the tract house. There he found the little kerosene brazier he'd once bought for a camping trip he'd never taken. After eating a can of salmon and half a jar of black olives, he made a bracket of wire for the brazier, bending its ends into hooks. That finished, Charley sat on the davenport wearing his ski suit and socks, waiting for full dark.

It was past ten when he had the balloon strung up on its rope over the brick barbecue and stood tending the coals. Occasionally he glanced up at the balloon watching its sides unwrinkle, puff out, and gradually swell into roundness. Then he heard some slight sound, a sigh or little movement. Eyes squinting, he searched the blackness, then found the faint blur of a face a dozen yards out in the night. But even before he found it, he knew who it would be. And when she knew he'd found her, Mrs. Lanidas walked slowly toward him and Charley saw a movement at her feet, a sudden dilution of the darkness, and realized that her dog was with her and had sat silently watching him, too.

In her tan polo coat, Mrs. Lanidas walked into the little circle of firelight and for a moment they stood staring at each other. "I've got to go up, too," she said quickly and desperately. "I want to come with you. Please. I've got to. I've simply got to. You must take me. Please!"

She continued, the words spilling out, and all the reasons for refusing came rising up in Charley's mind. But he didn't speak any of them; he knew the truth when he heard it. For whatever reasons—and what they were didn't matter—she, too, had to do what he'd known he must do the day he lay out here staring at the hawk in the sky. And because Charley understood that feeling of absolute necessity, he couldn't refuse it and didn't bother going through the motions of protest. He said, "All right," then gestured at the dog. "What about him?"

"I'll tie him up here. He'll sit quietly." She spoke anxiously, afraid he'd change his mind. "I'm out with him every night, sometimes till one, two, even three o'clock. My husband never waits up or even notices I'm gone. He'll never know."

"It's dangerous." Charley glanced up at the balloon but he spoke perfunctorily, and she simply nodded to acknowledge that she'd heard and accepted the warning.

The balloon was puffed tight now and tugging hard. Charley turned off the blower switch, then threw a bucket of water onto the coals and the cloud of smoke turned milk-white in the moonlight. He hooked the wire bracket holding the kerosene burner into the netting and the brazier hung under the open neck of the balloon several feet below it. Charley lighted it, then thrust the stovepipe up into the balloon neck and let it slide down over the brazier and now the heat from the intense blue flame poured up into the balloon.

Mrs. Lanidas had tied her dog's leash to the barbecue and he lay on the patio watching them, head cocked. Charley gestured politely at the swinglike seat hanging just over the flagstones. Mrs. Lanidas nodded, took off her coat, and Charley saw that she was not, as he'd thought, wearing black stockings; Mrs. Lanidas had on a skintight black leotard.

She sat down on the bar, holding the support rope, legs straight out over the pavement, ankles gracefully crossed. Charley sat beside her, glanced at her, and she nodded. He pulled at the rope and they rose instantly into the moonlight.

They rose swiftly, the houses, street, and hills contracting beneath them, and when he looked at Mrs. Lanidas the fear was gone from her eyes. They were half closed in pleasure now, the breeze rippling her hair, and she smiled at Charley in delight and he grinned back. Tonight the balloon didn't drift. Somewhere above hilltop level a high-up breeze took them, carrying them south, the balloon slowly revolving. As it turned Charley watched Mrs. Lanidas's face. She caught sight of the Bay, a vast blackness striped by moonlight, and of the jewel-bright orange dots of the bridge lights, and of the clustered white towers of the lighted city rising in splendor beyond the black water, and she gasped in pleasure and said, "Oh, my god!" and Charley laughed aloud, his pleasure reinforced by hers. The balloon completed its revolutions, and, their backs to the Bay now, they moved over the land watching it slide out from under their feet.

Marin County, California, is low softly rounded hills and little valleys winding between them; and it is flatland, seashore, and bay shore. It is towns with apartment buildings and not enough parking space and it is still-untouched areas where foxes and deer live. It is rows of squeezed-together tract houses, a commuting area; and there are ranches yet where real cowboys round up cattle. It has a mountain twenty-five hundred feet high, a forest of giant redwood trees, and there are miles of coastline on which ocean waves break. Soundlessly, effortlessly, they moved over this patchwork and Charley kept his bearings by the tiny moving lights on the highway that cut through the hills below. Sometimes he spilled sand from the paper ballast sacks strung in the netting beside him. Sometimes he released hot air from a vent in the top of the balloon or raised or lowered the flame in his burner. He had the feel of ballooning now. Moving steadily along through the sky and the night he had never, not even as a child, felt so free.

Off to the right lay the floodlighted buff-color walls of San Quentin Prison looking like a miniature castle. Behind it the lights of San Rafael lay scattered on its hills. Below them lay moon-washed darkness, an area unbuilt upon. It was glorious moving along above it; a thrill glowed in Charley's breast. At the same time it was an utter contentment, and glancing at Mrs. Lanidas beside him—who turned to smile—he knew she felt the same way. The air was soft and warm and pressed gently against their faces. He glanced over his shoulder; the great Bay, though still far ahead, was appreciably closer and Charley lowered the balloon feeling the decrease in pressure of the bar under his legs as they began sliding closer to the ground in a long, slow arc. The breeze held and Charley lowered again till they were perhaps a hundred feet above ground so that he could descend quickly if he had to before they were blown out over the Bay.

Swinging on their bar they crossed the boundary of a tract such as the one they lived in. From here it was a crisscross of sparsely illuminated streets; of squares of darkness that were front or back yards; of lighted windows; of rods of moving light which were automobiles; and of occasional rectangles of moonlight which were swimming pools. Sound moved up to them distinctly. The night was balmy, windows were open, and they heard—glancing at each other to smile—the familiar nightly blasts of gunfire from television sets. They crossed a back yard and saw the red glow of cigarette ends and the quiet voices of two men.

"Four kids named Stephen in his grade alone. Aren't there any kids named George or Frank any more?"

"I know. Same with girls, these days. Ten million Debbies and no more Ednas."

"Or Edwins."

"Or Gladyses."

"Or . . ."

They heard a child call, "Mom!" and the mother answer. "What is it? Now, get to sleep!" As a dog glanced up at the moon they saw the moonlight eerily reflected in its eyes. Then the dog saw the balloon's black silhouette moving across the face of the moon and raced the length of the back yard, its chain rattling, barking at them. Then for miles around and minutes afterward the barking was picked up and repeated like a tom-tom message. Not ten feet off in the darkness they heard a duck honk and the beat of its wings.

Charley felt godlike, drifting soundlessly and invisibly over the rooftops. He wondered what the people under them were doing and thinking. He loved them, suddenly, all of them, and wanted to bestow a blessing on them and did so. He trickled a little sand into his palm, then scattered it benevolently over the community below saying, "Blessings. Blessings on you all, from your friends Charley Burke and Mrs. Lanidas."

Then they laughed and in simultaneous impulse lifted their feet, ankles together, legs straight out, and leaned far back at arm's length, their free arms around each other's waists, supporting each other, and began to pump together, like children on a school playground. Alternately tucking their legs far back under their perch, then shooting them forward and up in unison, they swung back and forth in a great arc under the balloon and Charley began singing. "Come, Josephine, in my flying machine!" he shouted. "And it's *up* we'll go, *up* we'll go!" A man in pajamas hurried out into a yard directly below them, head turning rapidly as he looked all around. But he never looked up at Charley and Mrs. Lanidas grinning a hundred feet over his head and moving silently past.

They moved with the breeze, dipping with it into the valleys, then riding it over the hills again. They did this now, riding up the slope of a hill higher than any others they'd passed so far. They had left the tract, and the area below them was black and lightless. The balloon had revolved several times as they traveled so Charley was confused, not sure where they were, and when they reached the crest of the hill and rose over it the whole sweep of the Bay suddenly lay before them. Down the other slope, they moved with the breeze and an instant later sailed out across the shoreline over the Bay—and the enormous length and tremendous height of the great Golden Gate Bridge suddenly dwarfed them, towering over their heads and incredibly close, not fifty yards to the right.

And they were dropping. Here over the water the current of air that carried them flowed on down to the water's surface, moving just over it, and in the blackness beneath them Charley suddenly saw the white caps of waves. Then he heard them, too, heard their cold and watery ripple, and understood how very close they were. High, high overhead hung the roadway of the bridge, its yellow lighting shining far up into the shadowed red superstructure of towers and cables even farther beyond them. An instant later, arms tight around each other's waists, gripping the support ropes, they were staring directly up at the underside of the bridge, silhouetted blackly against the moonlit sky, and Charley understood that they were being swept under the bridge and out to sea, dangling just above the white-speckled black water.

He spilled ballast. He tore open the sand sacks as fast as his free arm could move. Their trapeze seat jerked under them, and they shot toward the sky. Kicking his feet sideways, gripping both ropes and jerking his body at the waist, Charley managed to turn the balloon so that they faced the bridge. But even before the half-turn was complete they'd shot to the level of the roadway and for an instant—not a dozen feet out in the blackness west of the bridge—they stared over their shoulders directly into the windows of cars driving past them. Then, Mrs. Lanidas clinging with one arm to Charley's waist, they were staring down at moving car roofs, yellowed by the bridge lights, and the car roofs were shrinking and they were still rising.

But now they were free of the surface breeze and climbing vertically. Even in his rigidly suppressed panic Charley was observing, judging. They rose but more and more slowly until—just higher than the flat tops of the enormous bridge towers—they stopped and through several moments hung absolutely motionless not six feet from the northern tower of the bridge and nearly level with its top. Far below the cars had shrunk to miniatures, the six-lane roadway to the width of a man's hand. Around them the air lay still and unmoving through a dozen heartbeats while they held their breaths. Then they felt the air stir infinitesimally, and ever so slowly it began to move them not seaward but back toward the bridge and for an instant Charley closed his eyes in relief. Then he opened them quickly to grin at Mrs. Lanidas and after a moment she smiled back.

Almost precisely even with the level top of the bridge tower, they drifted slowly toward it and would have bumped gently into it if Charley hadn't fended them off with his free arm. For a moment the flat top of the great bridge tower lay directly before them like a moonlit table top, their knees almost touching it. Inspired by the excitement of relief, Charley reached overhead and rubbed a finger across the base of the kerosene brazier. It came away blackened with soot and he leaned forward slightly and in the moonlight wrote "C.B." on the very top of the northern tower of the Golden Gate Bridge. He looked at it for a moment—proudly, smiling—then glanced at Mrs. Lanidas, and she reached up to the brazier, then wrote "E.L." just under his initials. Once more Mrs. Lanidas rubbed her finger through the soot of the brazier, reached out to the tower, and began to draw something—a circle, an oval, or something else—around the set of initials. But what it was to be Charley never knew because the breeze had them again now, their moment of motionlessness over, and they moved on across the bridge leaving their initials on its very top to the eternal mystification of the steeplejacks who painted it.

They were out over the Bay moving high above it in a wide arc that was carrying them, Charley saw, north toward the Marin County shoreline again. Off to the right lay the shining city and they stared down at it in awe. Its lights were scattered thinly now, most of the city asleep. But they picked out the floodlighted front of the Fairmont Hotel and, directly across from it at their own eye level, the huge windows of the Top of the Mark. Far to the south they saw Market Street angling across the city, the great dark rectangle of Golden Gate Park, and the whole maplike crisscrossing of San Francisco's streets rising over and then slipping down its hills. And they heard—very clearly—the toylike cling-clang of a cable-car bell.

Then they were across the shoreline moving almost due north in a straight line which, Charley saw, would intersect their mile-and-a-half-long east-and-west street. Almost sleepily now, they simply sat waiting until they should reach it. Presently, when he recognized the curving pattern of lighted dots ahead which were the lamps of their street, they moved along it, following the curving white center line toward home.

In the morning Charley's wife and daughter were back again, the house alive and happy once more. In the days, then weeks, then months that followed, he thought of his balloon packed away in the garage, and of using it again. But he never did and presently he realized that, alone no longer, he wasn't going to; that he'd had what he wanted from it and needed no more. And that, in fact, his flight in the balloon could not ever really be repeated. He thought of showing the balloon to his wife and of telling her what had happened. But he realized that he wasn't sure he knew what had happened; that what had happened was very little a matter of fact and almost entirely a matter of emotion for which he had no words.

He didn't see Mrs. Lanidas again for six months. Then he was at a P.T.A. meeting, and, the meeting over, the parents standing in the corridor chatting, Charley stood beside his wife who was talking to someone. He'd spoken politely to a number of people whom he saw nowhere else but here. His wife had introduced him to still others. Now he stood absently waiting, wanting to go home and have a drink. When his wife touched his arm, saying, "Charley, I want you to meet"—he turned with an automatic smile as she finished—"Mrs. Lanidas, from our street."

For a moment Charley stood looking at her knowing that, factually speaking, this was Mrs. Lanidas. Yet it wasn't at all. This was no laughing girl in a black leotard, sailing through the sky and the night as the wind rippled her hair. This was a mother of small children with the first lines in her face, all dressed up in a hat, good dress, dark coat, and wearing a girdle. Charley nodded pleasantly. "Oh, yes," he said politely, "I've met Mrs. Lanidas."

At the absurdity of this, she smiled, and for a moment—eyes warm, almost mischievous—she was a girl once more. Speaking to both of them, but her hand rising to touch Charley's sleeve, she said, "Not Mrs. Lanidas. Call me Josephine."

Out in the dark schoolyard as they got into their car, Charley's wife said, "Now, why did she say that? I'm almost certain her name isn't Josephine. I think it's Edna."

But Charley didn't answer. Sliding under the steering wheel he simply shrugged, smiling a little, and, half under his breath, he continued his whistling of an old, old tune.

Second Chance

I can't tell you, I know, how I got to a time and place no one else in the world even remembers. But maybe I can tell you how I felt the morning I stood in an old barn off the county road, staring down at what was to take me there.

I paid out seventy-five dollars I'd worked hard for after classes last semester—I'm a senior at Poynt College in Hylesburg, Illinois, my home town—and the middle-aged farmer took it silently, watching me shrewdly, knowing I must be out of my mind. Then I stood looking down at the smashed, rusty, rat-gnawed, dust-covered, old wreck of an automobile lying on the wood floor where it had been hauled and dumped thirty-three years before—and that now belonged to me. And if you can remember the moment, whenever it was, when you finally got something you wanted so badly you dreamed about it—then maybe I've told you how I felt staring at the dusty mass of junk that was a genuine Jordan Playboy.

You've never heard of a Jordan Playboy, if you're younger than forty, unless you're like I am; one of those people who'd rather own a 1926 Mercer convertible sedan, or a 1931 Packard touring car, or a '24 Wills Sainte Claire, or a '31 air-cooled

Franklin convertible—or a Jordan Playboy—then the newest, two-toned, '56 model made; I was actually half sick with excitement.

And the excitement lasted; it took me four months to restore that car, and that's fast. I went to classes till school ended for the summer, then I worked, clerking at J. C. Penney's; and I had dates, saw an occasional movie, ate and slept. But all I really did—all that counted—was work on that car; from six to eight every morning, for half an hour at lunchtime, and from the moment I got home, most nights, till I stumbled to bed, worn out.

My folks live in the big old house my dad was born in; there's a barn off at the back of the lot, and I've got a chain hoist in there, a workbench, and a full set of mechanic's tools. I built hot rods there for three years, one after another; those charcoal-black mongrels with the rear ends up in the air. But I'm through with hot rods; I'll leave those to the high-school set. I'm twenty years old now, and I've been living for the day when I could soak loose the body bolts with liniment, hoist the body aside, and start restoring my own classic. That's what they're called; those certain models of certain cars of certain years which have something that's lasted, something today's cars don't have for us, and something worth bringing back.

But you don't restore a classic by throwing in a new motor, hammering out the dents, replacing missing parts with anything handy, and painting it chartreuse. "Restore" means what it says, or ought to. My Jordan had been struck by a train, the man who sold it to me said—just grazed, but that was enough to flip it over, tumbling it across a field, and the thing was a wreck; the people in it were killed. So the right rear wheel and the spare were hopeless wads of wire spokes and twisted rims, and the body was caved in, with the metal actually split in places. The motor was a mess, though the block was sound. The upholstery was rat-gnawed, and almost gone. All the nickel plating was rusted and flaking off. And exterior parts were gone; nothing but screw holes to show they'd been there. But three of the wheels were intact, or almost, and none of the body was missing.

What you do is write letters, advertise in the magazines people like me read, ask around, prowl garages, junk heaps and barns, and you trade, and you bargain, and one way or another get together the parts you need. I traded a Winton name plate and hub caps, plus a Saxon hood, to a man in Wichita, Kansas, for two Playboy wheels, and they arrived crated in a wooden box—rusty, and some of the spokes bent and loose, but I could fix that. I bought my Jordan running-board mats and spare-wheel mount from a man in New Jersey. I bought two valve pushrods, and had the rest precision-made precisely like the others. And—well, I restored that car, that's all.

The body shell, every dent and bump gone, every tear welded and burnished down, I painted a deep green, precisely matching what was left of the old paint before I sanded it off. Door handles, windshield rim, and every other nickel-plated part, were restored, re-nickeled, and replaced. I wrote eleven letters to leather supply houses all over the country, enclosing sample swatches of the cracked old upholstery before I found a place that could match it. Then I paid a hundred and twelve dollars to have my Playboy reupholstered, supplying old photographs to show just how it should be done. And at eight ten one Saturday evening in July, I finally finished; my last missing part, a Jordan radiator cap, for which I'd traded a Duesenberg floor mat, had come from the nickel plater's that afternoon. Just for the fun of it, I put the old plates back on then; Illinois license 11,206, for 1923. And even the original ignition key, in its old leather case—oiled and worked supple again—was back where I'd found it, and now I switched it on, advanced the throttle and spark, got out with the crank, and started it up. And thirty-three years after it had bounced, rolled and crashed off a grade crossing, that Jordan Playboy was alive again.

I had a date, and knew I ought to get dressed; I was wearing stained dungarees and my dad's navy blue, high-necked old sweater. I didn't have any money with me; you lose it out of your pockets, working on a car. I was even out of cigarettes. But I couldn't wait, I had to drive that car, and I just washed up at the old sink in the barn, then started down the cinder driveway in that beautiful car, feeling wonderful. It wouldn't matter how I was dressed anyway, driving around in the Playboy tonight.

My mother waved at me tolerantly from a living room window, and called out to be careful, and I nodded; then I was out in the street, cruising along, and I wish you could have seen me—seen *it,* I mean. I don't care whether you've ever given a thought to the wonderful old cars or not, you'd have seen why it was worth all I'd done. Draw yourself a mental picture of a simple, straight-lined, two-seater, open automobile with four big wire wheels fully exposed, and its spare on the back in plain sight; don't put in a line that doesn't belong there, and have a purpose. Make the two doors absolutely square; what other shape should a door be? Make the hood perfectly rounded, louvered at the sides because the motor needs that ventilation. But don't add a single unnecessary curve, jiggle, squiggle, or porthole to that car—and picture the radiator, nothing concealing it and pretending it doesn't exist. And now see that Playboy as I did cruising along, the late sun slanting down through the big old trees along the street, glancing off the bright nickel so that it hurt your eyes,

the green of the body glowing like a jewel. It was beautiful, I tell you it was beautiful, and you'd think everyone would see that.

But they didn't. On Main Street, I stopped at a light, and a guy slid up beside me in a great big, shining, new '57 car half as long as a football field. He sat there, the top of the door up to his shoulders, his eyes almost level with the bottom of his windshield, looking as much in proportion to his car as a two-year-old in his father's overcoat; he sat there in a car with a pattern of chrome copied directly from an Oriental rug, and with a trunk sticking out past his back wheels you could have landed a helicopter on; he sat there for a moment, then turned, looked out, and smiled at *my* car!

And when I turned to look at him, eyes cold, he had the nerve to smile at *me,* as though I were supposed to nod and grin and agree that any car not made day before yesterday was an automatic side-splitting riot. I just looked away, and when the light changed, he thought he'd show me just how sick his big four-thousand-dollar job could make my pitiful old antique look. The light clicked, and his foot was on the gas, his automatic transmission taking hold, and he'd already started to grin. But I started when he did, feeding the gas in firm and gentle, and we held even till I shot into second faster than any automatic transmission yet invented can do it, and I drew right past him, and when I looked back it was me who was grinning. But still, at the next light, every pedestrian crossing in front of my car treated me to a tolerant understanding smile, and when the light changed, I swung off Main.

That was one thing that happened; the second was that my date wouldn't go out with me. I guess I shouldn't blame her. First she saw how I was dressed, which didn't help me with her. Then I showed her the Jordan at the curb, and she

nodded, not even slightly interested, and said it was very nice; which didn't help her with me. And then—well, she's a good-looking girl, Naomi Weygand, and while she didn't exactly put it in these words, she let me know she meant to be seen tonight, preferably on a dance floor, and not waste her youth and beauty riding around in some old antique. And when I told her I was going out in the Jordan tonight, and if she wanted to come along, fine, and if she didn't—well, she didn't. And eight seconds later she was opening her front door again, while I scorched rubber pulling away from the curb.

I felt the way you would have by then, and I wanted to get out of town and alone somewhere, and I shoved it into second, gunning the car, heading for the old Cressville road. It used to be the only road to Cressville, a two-lane paved highway just barely wide enough for cars to pass. But there's been a new highway for fifteen years; four lanes, and straight as a ruler except for two long curves you can do ninety on, and you can make the seven miles to Cressville in five minutes or less.

But it's a dozen winding miles on the old road, and half a mile of it, near Cressville, was flooded out once, and the concrete is broken and full of gaps; you have to drive it in low. So nobody uses the old road nowadays, except for four or five farm families who live along it.

When I swung onto the old road—there are a lot of big old trees all along it—I began to feel better. And I just ambled along, no faster than thirty, maybe, clear up to the broken stretch before I turned back toward Hylesburg, and it was wonderful. I'm not a sports-car man myself, but they've got something when they talk about getting close to the road and into the outdoors again—the way driving used to be before people shut themselves behind great sheets of glass and metal, and began rushing along super-highways, their eyes on the

white line. I had the windshield folded down flat against the hood, and the summer air streamed over my face and through my hair, and I could see the road just beside and under me flowing past so close I could have touched it. The air was alive with the heavy fragrances of summer darkness, and the rich nostalgic sounds of summer insects, and I wasn't even thinking, but just living and enjoying it.

One of the old Playboy advertisements, famous in their day, calls the Jordan "this brawny, graceful thing," and says, "It revels along with the wandering wind and roars like a Caproni biplane. It's a car for a man's man—that's certain. Or for a girl who loves the out of doors." Rich prose for these days, I guess; we're afraid of rich prose now, and laugh in defense. But I'll take it over a stern sales talk on safety belts.

Anyway, I liked just drifting along the old road, a part of the summer outdoors and evening, and the living country around me; and I was no more thinking than a collie dog with his nose thrust out of a car, his eyes half closed against the air stream, enjoying the feeling human beings so often forget, of simply being a living creature. " 'I left my love in Avalon,' " I was bawling out at the top of my lungs, hardly knowing when I'd started, " 'and saaailed awaaay!' " Then I was singing "Alice Blue Gown," very softly and gently. I sang, "Just a Japanese Saaandman!," and "Whispering," and "Barney Google," the fields and trees and cattle, and sometimes an occasional car, flowing past in the darkness, and I was having a wonderful time.

The name "Dempsey" drifted into my head, I don't know why—just a vagrant thought floating lazily up into my consciousness. Now, I saw Jack Dempsey once; six years ago when I was fourteen, my dad, my mother, and I took a vacation trip to New York. We saw the Empire State Building, Rockefeller Center, took a ride on the subway, and all the rest of it. And we had dinner at Jack Dempsey's restaurant on Broadway, and he was there, and spoke to us, and my dad talked to him for a minute about his fights. So I saw him; a nice-looking middle-aged man, very big and broad. But the picture that drifted up into my mind now, driving along the old Cressville road, wasn't that Jack Dempsey. It was the face of a young man not a lot older than I was, black-haired, black-bearded, fierce and scowling. Dempsey, I thought, that snarling young face rising up clear and vivid in my mind, and the thought completed itself: He beat Tom Gibbons last night.

Last night; Dempsey beat Gibbons *last night*—and it was true. I mean it *felt* true somehow, as though the thought were in the very air around me, like the old songs I'd found myself singing, and suddenly several things I'd been half aware of clicked together in my mind. I'd been dreamily and unthinkingly realizing that there were more cars on the road than I'd have expected, flowing past me in the darkness. Maybe some of the farm families along here were having some sort of Saturday-night get-together, I thought. But then I knew it wasn't true.

Picture a car's headlights coming toward you; they're two sharp beams slicing ahead into the darkness, an intense blue-white in color, their edges as defined as a ruler's. But these headlights—two more sets of them were approaching me now—were different. They were entirely orange in color, the red-orange of the hot filaments that produced them; and they were hardly even beams, but just twin circles of wide, diffused orange light, and they wavered in intensity, illuminating the road only dimly.

The nearer lights were almost upon me, and I half rose from my seat, leaning forward over the hood of the Jordan, staring at the car as it passed me. It was a Moon; a cream-colored nineteen-twenty-two Moon roadster.

The next car, those two orange circles of wavering light swelling, approached, then passed, as I stared and turned to look after it. It looked something like mine; wire wheels, but with the spare on a side mount, and with step plates instead of running boards. I knew what it was; a Haynes Speedster, and the man at the wheel wore a cloth cap, and the girl beside him wore a large pink hat, coming well down over her head, and with a wide brim all around it.

I sat moving along, a hand on the wheel, in a kind of stunned ecstatic trance. For now, the Saturday-night traffic at its peak, there they all came one after another, all the glorious old cars; a Saxon Six black-bodied touring car with wood-spoke wheels, and the women in that car wore chin-length veils from the edges of their flowered hats; there passed a gray-bodied black-topped Wills Sainte Claire with orange disc wheels, and the six kids in it were singing "Who's Sorry Now?" then I saw another Moon, a light blue open four-seater, its cut-out open, and the kid at the wheel had black hair slicked back in a varnished pompadour, and just glancing at him, you could see he was on his way to a date; now there came an Elcar, two Model T Fords just behind it; then a hundred yards back, a red Buick roadster with natural-wood spoke wheels; I saw a Velie, and a roadster that was either a Noma or a Kissel, I couldn't be sure; and there was a high-topped blue Dodge sedan with cut flowers in little glass vases by the rear doors; there was a car I didn't know at all; then a brand-new Stanley Steamer, and just behind it, a wonderful low-slung 1921 Pierce-Arrow, and I knew what had happened, and where I was.

I've read some of the stuff about Time with a capital T, and I don't say I understand it too well. But I know Einstein or somebody compares Time to a winding river, and says we exist as though in a boat, drifting along between high banks.

All we can see is the present, immediately around us. We can't see the future just beyond the next curve, or the past in the many bends in back of us. But it's all there just the same. There—countless bends back, in infinite distance—lies the past, as real as the moment around us.

Well, I'll join Einstein and the others with a notion of my own; just a feeling, actually, hardly even a thought. I wonder if we aren't barred from the past by a thousand invisible chains. You can't drive into the past in a 1957 Buick because there are no 1957 Buicks in 1923; so how could you be there in one? You can't drive into 1923 in a Jordan Playboy, along a four-lane superhighway; there are no superhighways in 1923. You couldn't even, I'm certain, drive with a pack of modern filter-tip cigarettes in your pocket—into a night when no such thing existed. Or with so much as a coin bearing a modern date, or wearing a charcoal-gray and pink shirt on your back. All those things, small and large, are chains keeping you out of a time when they could not exist.

But my car and I—the way I felt about it, anyway—were almost *rejected* that night, by the time I lived in. And so there in my Jordan, just as it was the year it was new, with nothing about me from another time, the old '23 tags on my car, and moving along a highway whose very oil spots belonged to that year—well, I think that for a few moments, all the chains hanging slack, we were free on the surface of Time. And that moving along that old highway through the summer evening, we simply *drifted*—into the time my Jordan belonged in.

That's the best I can do, anyway; it's all that occurs to me. And—well, I wish I could offer you proof. I wish I could tell you that when I drove into Hylesburg again, onto Main Street, that I saw a newspaper headline saying, PRESIDENT HARDING STRICKEN, or something like that. Or that I heard people discussing Babe Ruth's new home-run record, or saw a bunch of cops raiding a speak-easy.

But I saw or heard nothing of the sort, nothing much different from the way it always has been. The street was quiet and nearly empty, as it is once the stores shut down for the weekend. I saw only two people at first; just a couple walking along far down the street. As for the buildings, they've been there, most of them, since the Civil War, or before—Hylesburg's an old town—and in the semidarkness left by the street lamps, they looked the same as always, and the street was paved with brick as it has been since World War I.

No, all I saw driving along Main Street were—just little things. I saw a shoe store, its awning still over the walk, and that awning was striped; broad red and white stripes, and the edges were scalloped. You just don't see awnings like that, outside of old photographs, but there it was, and I pulled over to the curb, staring across the walk at the window. But all I can tell you is that there were no open-toed shoes among the women's, and the heels looked a little high to me, and a little different in design, somehow. The men's shoes—well, the toes seemed a little more pointed than you usually see now, and there were no suede shoes at all. But the kids' shoes looked the same as always.

I drove on, and passed a little candy and stationery shop, and on the door was a sign that said, *Drink Coca-Cola,* and in some way I can't describe the letters looked different. Not much, but—you've seen old familiar trademarks that have gradually changed, kept up to date through the years, in a gradual evolution. All I can say is that this old familiar sign looked a little different, a little old-fashioned, but I can't really say how.

There were a couple of all-night restaurants open, as I drove along, one of them The New China, the other Gill's, but they've both been in Hylesburg for years. There were a couple of people in each of them, but I never even thought of going in. It seemed to me I was here on sufferance, or by accident; that I'd just drifted into this time, and had no right to actually intrude on it. Both restaurant signs were lighted, the letters formed by electric-light bulbs, unfrosted so that you could see the filaments glowing, and the bulbs ended in sharp glass spikes. There wasn't a neon sign, lighted or unlighted, the entire length of the street.

On West Main I came to the Orpheum, and though the box office and marquee were dark, there were a few lights still on, and a dozen or so cars parked for half a block on each side of it. I parked mine directly across the street beside a wood telephone pole. Brick pavement is bumpy, and when I shut off the motor, and reached for the hand brake—I don't know whether this is important or not, but I'd better tell it—the Jordan rolled ahead half a foot as its right front wheel settled into a shallow depression in the pavement. For just a second or so, it rocked a little in a tiny series of rapidly decreasing arcs, then stopped, its wheel settled snugly into the depression as though it had found exactly the spot it had been looking for—like a dog turning around several times before it lies down in precisely the right place.

Crossing over to the Orph, I saw the big posters in the shallow glass showcases on each side of the entrance. *Fri., Sat., and Sun.,* one said, and it showed a man with a long thin face, wearing a monocle, and his eyes were narrowed, staring at a woman with long hair who looked sort of frightened. George Arliss, said the poster, in "The Green Goddess."

Coming Attraction, said the other poster, *Mon., Tues. and Wed.* "Ashes of Vengeance," starring Norma Talmadge and Conway Tearle, with Wallace Beery. I've never heard of any of them, except Wallace Beery. In the little open lobby, I looked at the still pictures in wall cases at each side of the box office; small, glossy, black and white scenes from the two movies, and finally recognized Wallace Beery, a thin, handsome, young man. I've never seen that kind of display before, and didn't know it was done.

But that's about all I can tell you; nothing big or dramatic, and nothing significant, like hearing someone say, "Mark my words, that boy Lindbergh will fly the Atlantic yet." All I saw was a little, shut-down, eleven-o'clock Main Street.

The parked cars, though, were a Dort; a high, straight-lined Buick sedan with wood wheels; three Model T's; a blue Hupmobile touring car with blue and yellow disc wheels; a Winton; a four-cylinder Chevrolet roadster; a Stutz; a spoke-wheeled Cadillac sedan. Not a single car had been made later than the year 1923. And this is the strange thing; they looked *right* to me. They looked as though that were the way automobiles were supposed to look, nothing odd, funny, or old-fashioned about them. From somewhere in my mind, I know I could have brought up a mental picture of a glossy, two-toned, chromium-striped car with power steering. But it would have taken a real effort, and—I can't really explain this, I know—it was as though modern cars didn't really exist; not yet. *These* were today's cars, parked all around me, and I knew it.

I walked on, just strolling down Main Street, glancing at an occasional store window, enjoying the incredible wonder of being where I was. Then, half a block or so behind me, I heard a sudden little babble of voices, and I looked back and the movie was letting out. A little crowd of people was flowing slowly out onto the walk to stand, some of them, talking for a moment; while others crossed the street, or walked on. Motors began starting, the parked cars pulling out from the curb, and I heard a girl laugh.

I walked on three or four steps maybe, and then I heard a sound, utterly familiar and unmistakable, and stopped dead in my tracks. My Jordan's motor had caught, roaring up as someone advanced the spark and throttle, and dying to its chunky, revving-and-ticking-over idle. Swinging around on the walk, I saw a figure, a young man's, vague and shadowy down the street, hop into the front seat, and then—the cut-out open—my Jordan shot ahead, tires squealing, down the street toward me.

I was frozen; I just stood there stupidly, staring at my car shooting toward me, my brain not working; then I came to life. It's funny; I was more worried about my car, about the way it was treated, than about the fact that it was being stolen. And I ran out into the street, directly into its path, my arms waving, and I yelled, "Hey! Take it easy!" The brakes slammed on, the Jordan skidding on the bricks, the rear end sliding sideways a little, and it slowed almost to a stop, then swerved around me, picking up speed again, and as I turned, following it with my eyes, I caught a glimpse of a girl's face staring at me, and a man my age at the wheel beside her, laughing, his teeth flashing white, and then they were past, and he yelled back, "You betcha! Take it easy; I always do!" For a moment I just stood staring after them, watching the single red tail-light shrinking into the distance; then I turned, and walked back toward the curb. A little part of the movie crowd was passing, and I heard a woman's voice murmur some question; then a man's voice, gruff and half angry, replied, "Yeah, of *course* it was Vince; driving like a fool as usual."

There was nothing I could do. I couldn't report a car theft to the police, trying to explain who I was, and where they could reach me. I hung around for a while, the street deserted once more, hoping they'd bring back my car. But they didn't, and finally I left, and just walked the streets for the rest of the night.

I kept well away from Prairie Avenue. If I was where I knew I was, my grandmother, still alive, was asleep in the big front bedroom of our house, and the thirteen-year-old in my room was the boy who would become my father. I didn't belong there now, and I kept away, up in the north end of town. It looked about as always; Hylesburg, as I've said, is old, and most of the new construction has been on the outskirts. Once in a while I passed a vacant lot where I knew there no longer was one; and when I passed the Dorsets' house where I played as a kid with Ray Dorset, it was only half built now, the wood of the framework looking fresh and new in the dark.

Once I passed a party, the windows all lighted, and they were having a time, noisy and happy, and with a lot of laughing and shrieks from the women. I stopped for a minute, across the street, watching; and I saw figures passing the lighted windows, and one of them was a girl with her hair slicked close to her head, and curving down onto her cheeks in sort of J-shaped hooks. There was a phonograph going, and the music—it was "China Boy"—sounded sort of distant, the orchestration tinny, and . . . different, I can't explain how. Once it slowed down, the tones deepening, and someone yelled, and then I heard the pitch rising higher again as it picked up speed, and knew someone was winding the phonograph. Then I walked on.

At daylight, the sky whitening in the east, the leaves of the big old trees around me beginning to stir, I was on Cherry Street. I heard a door open across the street, and saw a man in overalls walk down his steps, cut silently across the lawn, and open the garage doors beside his house. He walked in, I heard the motor start, and a cream and green '56 Oldsmobile backed out—and I turned around then, and walked on toward Prairie Avenue and home, and was in bed a couple hours before my folks woke up Sunday morning.

I didn't tell anyone my Jordan was gone; there was no way to explain it. Ed Smiley, and a couple other guys, asked me about it, and I said I was working on it in my garage. My folks didn't ask; they were long since used to my working on a car for weeks, then discovering I'd sold or traded it for something else to work on.

But I wanted—I simply had to have—another Playboy, and it took a long time to find one. I heard of one in Davenport, and borrowed Jim Clark's Hudson, and drove over, but it wasn't a Playboy, just a Jordan, and in miserable shape anyway.

It was a girl who found me a Playboy; after school started up in September. She was in my Economics IV class, a sophomore I learned, though I didn't remember seeing her around before. She wasn't actually a girl you'd turn and look at again, and remember, I suppose; she wasn't actually pretty, I guess you'd have to say. But after I'd talked to her a few times, and had a Coke date once, when I ran into her downtown—then she was pretty. And I got to liking her; quite a lot. It's like this; I'm a guy who's going to want to get married pretty early. I've been dating girls since I was sixteen, and it's fun, and exciting, and I like it fine. But I've just about had my share of that, and I'd been looking at girls in a different way lately; a lot more interested in what they were like than in just how good-looking they were. And I knew pretty soon that this was a girl I could fall in love with, and marry, and be happy with. I won't be fooling around with old cars all my life; it's just a hobby, and I know it, and I wouldn't expect a girl to get all interested in exactly how the motor of an old Marmon works. But I would expect her to take some interest in how I feel about old cars. And she did—Helen McCauley, her name is. She really did; she understood what I was talking about, and it wasn't faked either, I could tell.

So one night—we were going to the dance at the Roof Garden, and I'd called for her a little early, and we were sitting out on her lawn in deck chairs killing time—I told her how I wanted one certain kind of old car, and why it had to be just that car. And when I mentioned its name, she sat up, and said, "Why, good heavens, I've heard about the Playboy from Dad all my life; we've got one out in the barn; it's a beat-up old mess, though. Dad!" she called, turning to look up at the porch where her folks were sitting. "Here's a man you've been looking for!"

Well, I'll cut it short. Her dad came down, and when he heard what it was all about, Helen and I never did get to the dance. We were out in that barn, the old tarpaulin pulled off his Jordan, and we were looking at it, touching it, sitting in it, talking about it, and quoting Playboy ads to each other for the next three hours.

It wasn't in bad shape at all. The upholstery was gone; only wads of horsehair, and strips of brittle old leather left. The body was dented, but not torn. A few parts, including one headlight, and part of the windshield mounting, were gone, and the motor was a long way from running, but nothing serious. And all the wheels were there, and in good shape, though they needed renickeling.

Mr. McCauley gave me the car; wouldn't take a nickel for it. He'd owned that Jordan when he was young, had had it ever since, and loved it; he'd always meant, he said, to get it in running order again sometime, but knew he never would now. And once he understood what I meant about restoring a classic, he said that to see it and drive it again as it once was, was all the payment he wanted.

I don't know just when I guessed, or why; but the feeling

had been growing on me. Partly, I suppose, it was the color; the faded-out remains of the deep green this old car had once been. And partly it was something else, I don't know just what. But suddenly—standing in that old barn with Helen, and her mother and dad—suddenly I knew, and I glanced around the barn, and found them; the old plates nailed up on a wall, 1923 through 1931. And when I walked over to look at them, I found what I knew I would find; 1923 Illinois tag 11,206.

"Your old Jordan plates?" I said, and when he nodded, I said as casually as I could, "What's your first name, Mr. McCauley?"

I suppose he thought I was crazy, but he said, "Vincent. Why?"

"Just wondered. I was picturing you driving around when the Jordan was new; it's a fast car, and it must have been a temptation to open it up."

"Oh, yeah." He laughed. "I did that, all right; those were wild times."

"Racing trains; all that sort of thing, I suppose?"

"That's right," he said, and Helen's mother glanced at me curiously. "That was one of the things to do in those days. We almost got it one night, too; scared me to death. Remember?" he said to his wife.

"I certainly do."

"What happened?" I said.

"Oh"—he shrugged—"I was racing a train, out west of town one night; where the road parallels the Q tracks. I passed it, heading for the cross-road—you know where it is—that cuts over the tracks. We got there, my arms started to move, to swing the wheel and shoot over the tracks in front of that engine—when I knew I couldn't make it." He shook his head. "Two three seconds more; if we'd gotten there just two seconds earlier, I'd have risked it, I'm certain, and we'd have been killed, I know. But we were just those couple seconds too late, and I swung that wheel straight again, and shot on down the road beside that train, and when I took my foot off the gas, and the engine rushed past us, the fireman was leaning out of the cab shaking his fist, and shouting something, I couldn't hear what, but it wasn't complimentary." He grinned.

"Did anything delay you that night," I said softly, "just long enough to keep you from getting killed?" I was actually holding my breath, waiting for his answer.

But he only shook his head. "I don't know," he said without interest. "I can't remember." And his wife said, "I don't even remember where we'd been."

I don't believe—I really don't—that my Jordan Playboy is anything more than metal, glass, rubber and paint formed into a machine. It isn't alive; it can't think or feel; it's only a car. But I think it's an especial tragedy when a young couple's lives are cut off for no other reason than the sheer exuberance nature put into them. And I can't stop myself from feeling, true or not true, that when that old Jordan was restored—returned to precisely the way it had been just before young Vince McCauley and his girl had raced a train in it back in 1923—when it had been given a second chance; it went back to the time and place, back to the same evening in 1923, that would give them a second chance, too. And so again, there on that warm July evening, actually there in the year 1923, they got into that Jordan, standing just where they'd parked it, to drive on and race that train. But trivial events can affect important ones following them— —how often we've all said: If only this or that had happened, everything would have turned out so differently. And this time it did, for now something was changed. This time on that 1923 July evening, someone dashed in front of their car, delaying them only two or three seconds. But Vince McCauley, then, driving on to race along beside those tracks, changed his mind about trying to cross them; and lived to marry the girl beside him. And to have a daughter.

I haven't asked Helen to marry me, but she knows I will; after I've graduated, and got a job, I expect. And she knows that I know she'll say yes. We'll be married, and have children, and I'm sure we'll be driving a modern hard-top car like everyone else, with safety catches on the doors so the kids won't fall out. But one thing for sure—just as her folks did thirty-two years before—we'll leave on our honeymoon in the Jordan Playboy.

Hey, Look at Me!

About six months after Maxwell Kingery died I saw his ghost walking along Miller Avenue in Mill Valley, California. It was two twenty in the afternoon, a clear sunny day, and I saw him from a distance which I later paced off; it was less than fifteen feet. There is no possibility that I was mistaken about who—or what—I saw, and I'll tell you why I'm sure.

My name is Peter Marks, and I'm the book editor of a San Francisco newspaper. I live in Mill Valley a dozen miles from San Francisco, and I work at home most days, from about nine till around two or three in the afternoon. My wife is likely to need something from the store by then, so I generally walk downtown, nearly always stopping in at Meier's bakery which has a lunch counter. Until he died, I often had coffee there with Max Kingery, and we'd sit at the counter for half an hour and talk.

He was a writer, so it was absolutely inevitable that I'd be introduced to him soon after he came to Mill Valley. A lot of writers live here, and whenever a new one arrives people love to introduce us and then stand back to see what will happen. Nothing much ever does, though once a man denounced me right out on the sidewalk in front of the Redhill liquor store. "Peter Marks? The book critic?" he said, and when I nodded he said, "You, sir, are a puling idiot who ought to be writing 'News of Our Pets' for the *Carmel Pine Cone* instead of criticizing the work of your betters." Then he turned, and—this is the word—stalked off, while I stood staring after him, smiling. I'd panned two of his books; he'd been waiting for Peter Marks ever since, and was admirably ready when his moment came.

But all Max Kingery said, stiffly, the day we were introduced, was, "How do you do," then he stood there nodding rapidly a number of times, finally remembering to smile; and that's all I said to him. It was in the spring, downtown in front of the bank, I think, and Max was bareheaded, wearing a light-brown, shabby-looking topcoat with the collar turned up. He was a black-haired, black-eyed man with heavy black-rimmed glasses, intense and quick-moving; it was hard for him to stand still there. He was young but already stooped, his hair thinning. I could see this was a man who took himself seriously but his name rang no bell in my mind and we spoke politely and parted quickly, probably forever if we hadn't kept meeting in the bakery after that. But we both came in for coffee nearly every afternoon, and after we'd met and nodded half a dozen times we were almost forced to sit together at the counter and try to make some conversation.

So we slowly became friends; he didn't have many. After I knew him I looked up what he'd written, naturally, and found it was a first novel which I'd reviewed a year before. I'd said it showed promise, and that I thought it was possible he'd write a fine novel some day, but all in all it was the kind of review usually called "mixed," and I felt awkward about it.

But I needn't have worried. I soon learned that what I or anyone else thought of his book was of no importance to Max;

he knew that in time I and everyone else would have to say that Maxwell Kingery was a very great writer. Right now not many people, even here in town, knew he was a writer at all but that was okay with Max; he wasn't ready for them to know. Some day not only every soul in Mill Valley but the inhabitants of remote villages in distant places would know he was one of the important writers of his time, and possibly of all time. Max never said any of this but you learned that he thought so and that it wasn't egotism. It was just something he knew, and maybe he was right. Who knows how many Shakespeares have died prematurely, how many young geniuses we've lost in stupid accidents, illnesses, and wars?

Cora, my wife, met Max presently, and because he looked thin, hungry, and forlorn—as he was—she had me ask him over for a meal, and pretty soon we were having him often. His wife had died about a year before we met him. (The more I learned about Max, the more it seemed to me that he was one of those occasional people who, beyond all dispute, are plagued by simple bad luck all their lives.) After his wife died and his book had failed, he moved from the city to Mill Valley, and now he lived alone working on the novel which, with the others to follow, was going to make him famous. He lived in a mean cheap little house he'd rented, walking downtown for meals. I never knew where he got whatever money he had; it wasn't much. So we had him over often so Cora could feed him, and once he was sure he was welcome he'd stop in of his own accord, if his work were going well. And nearly every day I saw him downtown, and we'd sit over coffee and talk.

It was seldom about writing. All he'd ever say about his own work when we met was that it was going well or that it was not, because he knew I was interested. Some writers don't like to talk about what they're doing, and he was one; I never even knew what his book was about. We talked about politics, the possible futures of the world, and whatever else people on the way to becoming pretty good friends talk about. Occasionally he read a book I'd reviewed, and we'd discuss it, and my review. He was always polite enough about what I did, but his real attitude showed through. Some writers are belligerent about critics, some are sullen and hostile, but Max was just contemptuous. I'm sure he believed that all writers outranked all critics—well or badly, they actually do the deed which we only sit and carp about. And sometimes Max would listen to an opinion of mine about someone's book, then he'd shrug and say, "Well, you're not a writer," as though that severely limited my understanding. I'd say, "No, I'm a critic," which seemed a good answer to me, but Max would nod as though I'd agreed with him. He liked me, but to Max my work made me only a hanger-on, a camp follower, almost a parasite. That's why it was all right to accept free meals from me; I was one of the people who live off the work writers do, and I'm sure he thought it was only my duty, which I wouldn't deny, to help him get his book written. Reading it would be my reward.

But of course I never read Max's next book or the others that were to follow it; he died that summer, absolutely pointlessly. He caught flu or something—one of those nameless things everyone gets occasionally. But Max didn't always eat well or live sensibly, and it hung on and turned into pneumonia, though he didn't know that. He lay in that little house of his waiting to get well, and didn't. By the time he got himself to a doctor, and the doctor got him to a hospital and got some penicillin in him, it was too late and Max died in Marin General Hospital that night.

What made it even more shocking to Cora and me was the way we learned about it. We were out of town on vacation six hundred miles away in Utah when it happened, and didn't know about it. (We've thought over and again, of course, that if only we'd been home when Max took sick we'd have taken him to our house and he'd never have gotten pneumonia, and I'm sure it's true; Max was just an unlucky man.) When we got home, not only did we learn that Max was dead but even his funeral, over ten days before, was already receding into the past.

So there was no way for Cora and me to make ourselves realize that Max was actually gone forever. You return from a vacation and slip back into an old routine so easily sometimes it hardly seems you'd left. It was like that now, and walking into the bakery again for coffee in the afternoons it seemed only a day or so since I'd last seen Max here, and whenever the door opened I'd find myself glancing up.

Except for a few people who remembered seeing me around town with Max, and who spoke to me about him now, shaking their heads, it didn't seem to me that Max's death was even discussed. I'm sure people had talked about it to some extent at least, although not many had known him well or at all. But other events had replaced that one by some days. So to Cora and me Max's absence from the town didn't seem to have left any discernible gap in it.

Even visiting the cemetery didn't help. It's in San Rafael, not Mill Valley, and the grave was in a remote corner; we had to climb a steep hill to reach it. But it hardly seemed real; there was no marker, and we had to count in from the road to even locate it. Standing there in the sun with Cora, I felt a flash of resentment against his relatives, but then I knew I shouldn't. Max had a few scattered cousins or something in New Jersey and Pennsylvania. The last time he'd known any of them at all well they'd been children, and he hadn't corresponded with them since. Now they'd sent a minimum of money to California to pay expenses, more from family pride than for Max, I expect, and none of them had come themselves. You couldn't blame them, it was a long way and expensive, but it was sad; there'd been only five people at the funeral. Max had never been in or even seen this cemetery, and standing at the unmarked grave, the new grass already beginning, I couldn't get it through my head that it had anything much to do with him.

He just vanished from the town, that's all. His things—a half-finished manuscript, portable typewriter, a few clothes, and half a ream of unused yellow paper—had been shipped to his relatives. And Max, with a dozen great books hidden in his brain, who had been going to become famous, was now just gone, hardly missed and barely remembered.

Time is the great healer; it makes you forget; sometimes it makes you forget literally and with great cruelty. I knew a man whose wife ran away, and he never saw her again. He missed her so much he thought he could never for a moment forget it. A year later, reading in his living room at night, he became so absorbed in his book that when he heard a faint familiar noise in the kitchen he called out without looking up from his book and asked his wife to bring him a cup of tea when she came back into the room. Only when there was no answer did he look up from his complete forgetfulness; then his loss swept over him worse than ever.

About six months after Max died, I finished my day's work and walked downtown. This was in January, and we'd just had nearly a month of rain, fog, and wet chill. Then California did what it does several times every winter and for which I always forgive it anything. The rain stopped, the sun came out, the sky turned an unclouded blue, and the temperature went up into the high seventies. Everything was lush from the winter rains and there was no way to distinguish those three or four days from summer, and I walked into town in shirtsleeves. And when I started across Miller Avenue by the bus station heading for Meier's bakery across the street and saw Max Kingery over there walking toward the corner of Throckmorton just ahead, I wasn't surprised but just glad to see him. I think it was because this was like a continuation of the summer I'd known him, the interval following it omitted, and because I'd never really had proof that he died. So I walked on, crossing the street and watching Max, thin, dark and intense; he didn't see me. I was waiting till I got close enough to call to him and I reached the middle of the street and even took a step or two past it before I remembered that Max Kingery was dead. Then I just stood there, my mouth hanging open, as Max or what seemed to be Max walked on to the corner, turned, and moved on out of sight.

I went on to the bakery then and had my coffee; I had to have something. I don't know if I could have spoken but I didn't have to; they always set a cup of coffee in front of me when I come in. My hand shook when I lifted the cup, and I spilled some, and if it had occurred to me I'd have gone to a bar instead and had several drinks.

If you ever have some such experience you'll learn that people resist believing you as they resist nothing else; you'll resist it yourself. I got home and told Cora what had happened; we sat in the living room and this time I did have a drink in my hand. She listened; there really wasn't much to say, I found, except that I'd seen Max Kingery walking along Miller Avenue. I couldn't blame Cora; my words sounded flat and foolish as I heard them. She nodded and said that several times she'd seen dark, preoccupied, thin young men downtown who reminded her a little of Max. It was only natural; it was where we'd so often run into him.

Patiently I said, "No, listen to me, Cora. It's one thing to see someone who reminds you of someone else—from a distance, or from the back, or just as he disappears in a crowd. But you cannot possibly mistake a stranger when you see him close up and see his face in full daylight for someone you know well and saw often. With the possible exception of identical twins, there are no such resemblances between people. That was Max, Cora, Max Kingery and no one else in the world."

Cora just sat there on the davenport continuing to look at me; she didn't know what to say. I understood, and felt half sorry for her, half irritated. Finally—she had to say *something*—she said, "Well . . . what was he wearing?"

I had to stop and think. Then I shrugged. "Well, just some kind of pants; I didn't notice the shoes; a dark shirt of some kind, maybe plaid, I don't know. And one of those round straw hats."

"Round straw hats?"

"Yeah, you know. You see people wearing them in the summer. I think they buy them at carnivals or somewhere. With a peak. Shaped like a baseball cap, only they're made of some kind of shiny yellow straw. Usually the peak is stitched around the rim with a narrow strip of red cloth or braid. This one was, and it had a red button on top, and"—I remembered this suddenly, triumphantly—"it had his initials on front! Big red initials, M.K., about three inches high, stitched into the straw just over the peak in red thread or braid or something."

Cora was nodding decisively. "That proves it."

"Of course! It . . ."

"No, no," she said irritably. "It proves that it *wasn't* Max; it couldn't be!"

I don't know why we were so irritable; fear of the unnatural, I suppose. "And just how does it prove that?"

"Oh, Pete! Can you *imagine* Max Kingery of all people wearing a hat like that? You've got to be"—she shrugged, hunting for the word—"some kind of extrovert to wear silly hats. Of all people in the world who would *not* wear a straw baseball cap with a red button on the top and three-inch-high *initials* on the front . . ." She stopped, looking at me anxiously, and after a moment I had to agree.

"Yeah," I said slowly. "He'd be the last guy in the world to wear one of those." I gave in then; there wasn't anything else to do. "It must have been someone else. I probably got the initials wrong; I saw what I thought they ought to be instead of what they were. It would *have* to be someone else, naturally, cap or no cap." Then the memory of what I'd seen rose up in my mind again clear as a sharply detailed photograph, and I said slowly. "But I just hope you see him sometime, that's all. Whoever he is."

She saw him ten days later. There was a movie at the Sequoia we wanted to see, so we got our sitter, then drove downtown after supper; the weather was clear and dry but brisk, temperature in the middle or high thirties. When we got to the box office, the picture was still on with twenty minutes to go yet, so we took a little walk first.

Except for the theater and a bar or two, downtown Mill Valley is locked up and deserted at night. But most of the display windows are left lighted, so we strolled along Throckmorton Avenue and began looking into them, beginning with Gomez Jewelry. We were out of sight of the theater here, and as we moved slowly along from window to window there wasn't another human being in sight, not a car moving, and our own footsteps on the sidewalk—unusually loud—were the only sound. We were at the Men's Shop looking in at a display of cuff links, Cora urging me once more to start wearing shirts with French cuffs so I could wear links in my sleeves, when I heard footsteps turn a corner and begin approaching us on Throckmorton, and I knew it was Max.

I used to say that I'd like to have some sort of psychical experience, that I'd like to see a ghost, but I was wrong. I think it must be one of the worst kinds of fear. I now believe it can drive men insane and whiten their hair, and that it has. It's a nasty fear, you're so helpless, and it began in me now, increasing steadily, and I wanted to spare Cora the worst of it.

She was still talking, pointing at a pair of cuff links made from old cable-car tokens. I knew she would become aware of the footsteps in a moment and turn to see whoever was passing. I had to prepare her before she turned and saw Max full in the face without warning, and—not wanting to—I turned my head slowly. A permanent awning projects over the store fronts along here, and the light from the windows seemed to be confined under it, not reaching the outer edge of the walk beyond the awning. But there was a three-quarter moon just rising above the trees that surround the downtown area, and by that pale light I saw Max walking briskly along that outer edge of sidewalk beside the curb, only a dozen yards away now. He was bareheaded and I saw his face sharp and clear, and it was Max beyond all doubt. There was no way to say anything else to myself.

I slipped my hand under Cora's coat sleeve and began squeezing her upper arm, steadily harder and harder till it must have approached pain—and she understood, becoming aware of the footsteps. I felt her body stiffen and I wished she wouldn't but knew she had to—she turned. Then we stood there as he walked steadily toward us in the moonlight. My scalp stirred, each hair of my head moved and tried to stand. The skin all over my body chilled as the blood receded from it. Beside me Cora stood shivering, violently, and her teeth were chattering, the only time in my life I've ever heard the sound. I believe she would have fallen except for my grip on her arm.

Courage was useless, and I don't claim I had any, but it seemed to me that to save Cora from some unspeakable consequence of fear beyond ability to bear it that I had to speak and that I had to do it casually. I can't say why I thought that but as Max approached—his regular steadily advancing steps the only sound left in the world now, his white face in the moonlight not ten feet away—I said, "Hello, Max."

At first I thought he wasn't going to answer or respond in any way. He walked on, eyes straight ahead, for at least two more steps, then his head turned very slowly as though the effort were enormous, and he looked at us as he passed with a terrible sadness lying motionless in his eyes. Then, just as slowly, he turned away again, eyes forward, and he was actually a pace or two beyond us when his voice—a dead monotone, the effort tremendous—said, "Hello," and it was the voice of despair, absolute and hopeless.

The street curves just ahead—he would disappear around its bend in a moment—and, as I stared after him, in spite of the fear and sorrow for Max I was astounded at what I saw now. There is a kind of jacket which rightly or wrongly I associate with a certain kind of slouching, thumbs-hooked-in-the-belt juvenile exhibitionist. They are made of some sort of shiny sateenlike cloth, always in two bright and violently contrasting colors—the sleeves yellow, the body a chemical green, for example—and usually a name of some sort is lettered across its back. Teen-age gangs wear them, or used to.

Max wore one now. It was hard to tell colors in the moonlight but I think it was orange with red sleeves, and stitched on the back in a great flowing script that nearly covered it was

Max K. Then he was gone, around the corner, his fading footsteps continuing two, three, four, or five more times as they dwindled into silence.

I had to support Cora and her feet stumbled as we walked to the car. In the car she began to cry, rocking back and forth, her hands over her face. She told me later that she'd cried from grief at feeling such fear of Max. But it helped her, and I drove us to lights and people, to a crowded bar away from Mill Valley in Sausalito a few miles off. We sat and drank then, several brandies each, and talked and wondered and asked each other the same questions but had no answers.

I think other people saw Max in Mill Valley during those days. One of the local cab drivers who park by the bus station walked up to me one day; actually he strolled, hands in pockets, making a point of seeming very casual. He said, "Say, that friend of yours, that young guy used to be around town that died?" There was caution in his voice, and he stood watching me closely as I answered. I nodded and said yeah to show that I understood who he meant. "Well, did he have a brother or something?" the driver said, and I shook my head and said not that I knew of. He nodded but was unsatisfied, still watching my face and waiting for me to offer something more but I didn't. And I knew he'd seen Max. I'm sure others saw him and knew who it was, as Cora and I did; it isn't something you mention casually. And I suppose there were those who saw him and merely recognized him vaguely as someone they'd seen around town before.

I walked over to Max's old house a day or so after we'd seen him; by that time, of course, I knew why he'd come back. The real-estate office that had it listed for rental again would have let me have the key if I'd asked; they knew me. But I didn't know what I could tell them as a reason for going in. It was an old house, run down, too small for most people, not the kind that rents quickly or that anyone bothers guarding too diligently. I felt sure I could get in somewhere, and on the tiny back porch, shielded from view, I tried the kitchen window and it opened and I climbed in.

The few scraps of furniture that had come with the place were still there, in the silence: a wooden table and two chairs in the tiny kitchen which Max had hardly used; the iron single bed in the bedroom, the wornout musty-smelling davenport and matching chair in the living room, and the rickety card table beside the front windows where Max had worked. What little I found, I found lying on the floor beside the table: two crumpled-up wads of the yellow copy paper Max had used.

I opened them up but it's hard to describe what was written on them. There were single words and what seemed to be parts of words and fragments of sentences and completely unreadable scribblings, all written in pencil. There was a word that might have been "forest" or "foreign"; the final letters degenerated into a scrawl as though the hand holding the pencil had begun to fall away from the paper before it could finish. There was an unfinished sentence beginning, "She ran to," and the stroke crossing the *t* wavered on part way across and then down the sheet till it ran off the bottom. There is no use describing in detail what is on those two crumpled sheets; there's no sense to be made of it, though I've often tried. It looks, I imagine, like the scrawlings of a man weak from fever and in delirium, as though every squiggle and wobbly line were made with almost-impossible effort. And I'm sure they were. It is true that they might be notes jotted down months earlier when Max was alive and which no one bothered to pick up and remove; but I know they aren't. They're the reason Max came back. They're what he tried to do, and failed.

I don't know what ghosts are or why, in rare instances, they appear. Maybe all human beings have the power, if they have the will, to reappear as Max and a few others have done occasionally down through the centuries. But I believe that to do so takes some kind of terrible and unimaginable expenditure of psychic energy. I think it takes such a fearful effort of will that it is beyond our imagining, and that only very rarely is such an incredible effort made.

I think a Shakespeare killed before *Hamlet, Othello,* or *Macbeth* were written might have put forth such effort and returned. And I know that Max Kingery did. But there was almost nothing left over to do what he came back for. Those meaningless fragments were the utmost he could accomplish. His appearances were at the cost of tremendous effort, and I think that to even turn his head and look at us in addition, as he did the night we saw him, and then to actually pronounce an audible word besides, were efforts no one alive can understand.

It was beyond him; he could not return and then write the books that were to have made the name of Max Kingery what he'd been certain it was destined to be. And so he had to give up; we never saw Max again, though we saw one more place he'd been.

Cora and I were driving to San Rafael over the county road. You can get there on a six-lane highway now, 101, that slices straight through the hills, but this was once part of the only road between the two towns and it winds a lot around and between the Marin County hills, under the trees. It's a pleasant narrow little two-lane road, and we like to take it once in a while; I believe it's still the shortest route to San Rafael, winding though it is. This was the end of January or early in February, I don't remember. It was early in the week, I'd taken the day off, and Cora wanted something at Penney's, so we drove over.

Twenty or thirty feet up on the side of a hill about a mile outside Mill Valley there's an outcropping of smooth-faced rock facing the road, and Cora glanced at it, exclaimed and pointed, and I jammed on the brakes and looked up where she was pointing. There on the rock facing the public road, painted in great four-foot letters, was MAX KI, the lines crude and uneven, driblets of paint running down past the bottoms of letters, the final stroke continuing on down the face of the rock until the paint or oil on the brush or stick had run thin and faded away. We knew Max had painted it—his name or as much of it as he could manage—and staring up at it now, I understood the loud jacket with MAX K on its back, and the carnival straw hat with the big red initials.

For who *are* the people who paint their names or initials in public places and on the rocks that face our highways? Driving from San Francisco to Reno over the Donner Pass you see them by the hundreds, some painted so high that the rocks must have been scaled, dangerously, to do it. I used to puzzle over them; to paint your name or initials up there in the mountains wasn't impulse. It took planning. You'd have to drive over a hundred miles with the can of paint on the floor of the car. Who would do that? And who would wear the caps stitched with initials and the jackets with names on their backs? It was plain to me now; they are the people, of course, who feel that they have no identity. And who are fighting for one.

They are unknown, nearly invisible, so they feel; and their names or initials held up to the uninterested eyes of the world are silent shouts of, "Hey, look at me!" Children shout it incessantly while acquiring their identities, and if they never acquire one maybe they never stop shouting. Because the things they do must always leave them with a feeling of emptiness. Initials on their caps, names on their jackets, or even painted high on a cliff visible for miles, they must always feel their failure to leave a real mark, and so they repeat it again and again. And Max who had to be someone, who *had* to be, did as they did, finally, from desperation. To have never been anyone and to be forgotten completely was not to be borne. At whatever cost he too had to try to leave his name behind him even if he were reduced to painting it on a rock.

I visited the cemetery once more, that spring, plodding up the hill, eyes on the ground. Nearing the crest I looked up, then stopped in my tracks, astounded. There at the head of Max's grave stood an enormous gray stone, the biggest by far of any in sight, and it was made not of concrete or pressed stone but of the finest granite. It would last a thousand years, and cut deeply into its face in big letters was MAXWELL KINGERY, AUTHOR.

Down in his shop outside the gates I talked to the middle-aged stonecutter in the little office at the front of the building; he was wearing a work apron and cap. He said, "Yes, certainly I remember the man who ordered it—black hair and eyes, heavy glasses. He told me what it should say, and I wrote it down. Your name's Peter Marks, isn't it?" I said it was, and he nodded as though he knew it. "Yes, he told me you'd be here, and I knew you would. Hard for him to talk; had some speech impediment, but I understood him." He turned to a littered desk, leafed through a little stack of papers, then found the one he wanted, and slid it across the counter to me. "He said you'd be in, and pay for it; here's the bill. It's expensive but worth it, a fine stone and the only one here I know of for an author."

For several moments I just stood there staring at the paper in my hand. Then I did the only thing left to do, and got out one of the checks I carry in my wallet. Waiting while I wrote, the stonecutter said politely, "And what do you do, Mr. Marks; you an author, too?"

"No," I said, signing the check, then I looked up smiling. "I'm just a critic."

About the Author

Jack Finney is the much-admired, widely-praised author of classics like INVASION OF THE BODY SNATCHERS and TIME AND AGAIN. He lives in Northern California.